Advance
Our Time

"Forester captures San Francisco in a way few have—he gives us the grit, the excess and the adventure, but also the magic and wonder that made the city a once upon a time. It really is a very inspired piece of writing, so honest, so real."—Trebor Healey, author of *A Horse Named Sorrow*

"Chuck's romp through his coming out in 1970s San Francisco is more than just a single guy on the loose, it's the narrative of the building of a movement." —Jewelle Gomez, author of *The Gilda Stories*

"Chuck Forester adroitly captures the sexualized zeitgeist of San Francisco in the early 1970s, as gay men flocked there to find themselves, each other, and created new unabashed futures together." —John R. Killacky, Executive Director, Flynn Center for the Performing Arts

OUR TIME
San Francisco in the '70s

OUR TIME
San Francisco in the '70s

Chuck Forester

Querelle Press
New York, NY

Published by Querelle Press LLC
2808 Broadway, #4
New York, NY 10025

www.querellepress.com

ISBN 978-0-9967103-8-1, paper edition
ISBN 978-0-9967103-9-8, e-book edition

Printed in the United States
Cover design by Linda Kosarin/The Art Department
Typeset by Raymond Luczak

"Every hour of every day
is an unspeakably perfect miracle."
Walt Whitman

"We're all golden sunflowers inside."
Allen Ginsberg

Dedicated to the men of my generation lost to AIDS

AUTHOR'S NOTE

This story began in the 1950s, when San Francisco was an outpost of freaks. Gay service men liked what they saw before being shipped out to bases in the Pacific and others came to escape being hounded back home. They wrote glowing letters to their friends back home about holding hands in public. Their friends told their friends who told their friends who told their friends, so by 1971 every month another thousand gay men showed up at San Francisco's foggy doorstep ready to be live as openly gay men. The city left its communities to their own devices and that allowed us to reinvent ourselves as we took over the Castro and rewrote the meaning of exuberance.

As a kid, I read newspaper accounts of blacks being brutally beaten when they stood up to segregation. I watched urban riots burn swaths of Detroit and LA to rubble. I watched the demonstration at the Democratic Convention in Chicago in 1968 turn into a police riot. I was one of thousands that surrounded the Pentagon to protest the war in Vietnam, so I was a seasoned activist when I arrived in San Francisco.

The mainstream press wrote off the early '70s in San Francisco as an orgy of sex and drugs and I plead guilty. I indulged in all the sex I'd repressed and especially the kinky sex, because sex was the best way to make friends. I experimented with opium and crack cocaine and LSD toyed with my psyche; I smoke weed because it lets me be stupid, and San Francisco has been my home since 1971 and I've been an HIV/AIDS survivor since 1978.

The early '70s in San Francisco saw a coming together of our desire to have our own gay neighborhood, a city that welcomed outcasts, and because the middle class had abandoned the city, gay men brought vacant housing back to life in beautiful, imaginative ways and I knew unconditional love.

We crafted a sex-positive community in the Castro, and without knowing it we built the reservoir of strength we would nearly deplete when we dealt with AIDS. Thousands of extraordinary human beings died but my generation wrote the book on HIV-AIDS treatment and care. Eric Rofes, an activist friend, insisted I record this crucial pivot in our history because our generation was already dead or dying of AIDS. He said we were the only ones who could tell the story and most of us thought it would go on forever. Eric died in 2006. After working in government and non-profits I went back to school and got a degree in poetry. I considered writing this as a memoir but the breadth of the story suggested a novel. The characters are amalgams drawn from my incredible family of beautiful men. The hardest part was conveying our confidence in ourselves and my gratitude to San Francisco.

I've included a sound track of the music I heard as I invented myself as a gay man. If someone like Gus Van Sant makes the movie, millions will see extraordinary men do extraordinary things just by being themselves.

San Francisco 1971

ONE

I'd had enough! No more being the "sweet cute boy" hard cheese cocktail parties with their bitching and innuendoes that started when I was fifteen. No more of Mr. Trencher, our pastor with Christ on the wall, who let me do him, but once he came, and to take care of my own needs I had to go home. I wanted honest sex. Salvation came when I was awarded a Merit Scholarship and accepted at an Ivy League school. On a cool September day I packed as fast as I could and left expecting I'd never know another day of back-biting sex. Sadly, the gay men I met in Hanover were just as conflicted as the men back home and I dropped out. My cousin Kerry lived in San Francisco, and I'd always wanted to live in a big city, so I decided to join him. What I knew of San Francisco was sketchy, but its hippies and beats could talk about sex and not give a damn who heard them. There I could live openly as a gay man and when I imaged a life without the crap gay men in my small town heaped on each other it sent chills down my spine. I didn't know how to start a conversation with a man who knew more about sex than I did. I could deal with starting out there a loner because I'd been one since Father died when I was ten and I created my own life and had to trust myself. My greatest fear was not being able to please a man, but there I was at the O'Hare gate in a surplus store leather jacket and my 501s, Paul Edward Bullen, nineteen years old, with long auburn hair and adequate equipment, about to board the plane to paradise and I couldn't wipe the shit-eating grin off my face.

Life really started for me at noon on the corner of 18th Street and Castro Street. For the first time in my life Pacific breezes that messed with my already unruly hair and evening fog that erased the day's pain was mine. I had a life where instead of thinking of what I'd fucked up I was challenged to think without judgment about what made me special. In a split second, I went from being frightened someone might expose me as a queer to being told I was a lovely man. I used to wear clothing to protect me from the elements and the eyes of the hardworking, well-meaning people in Wisconsin who were uncomfortable around me because I wasn't quite like them but here exposing my body including my junk to the sun on a nude beach was a rite of passage. The closet I lived in for years was not just dark it was incredibly small and now I was standing at the corner of streets and the sidewalks from building to the curb were filled with more excited gay men than I thought existed in the entire world. Low expectations helped in Wisconsin because there wasn't much there, but here I wanted to dip into every pool, touch every man and exclaim to the world I am gay man. The change was so stark it felt like Alice falling through the looking glass and such a momentous change causes the timid to flee, but I was home.

The city was better than I expected, a half-naked man in a second story window was showing off to a friend while "American Pie" blasted from the speaker next to him. No sooner had I taken that in than I stumbled on two men holding hands on the curb. I grinned at something I couldn't believe; they were holding hands in public! I mumbled, "Sorry," and they smiled back. It kept getting better when I passed a café and a bearded man kissed the skinny kid he was with. I stared in disbelief! I'd never seen men kiss and I wanted to hug them, but I respected their privacy and looked away. Good looking men called out to each other from both sides of the street and I couldn't believe that many good-looking men even existed. They were everywhere

I looked. Even better, being gay didn't faze them. I wanted to be like them but I didn't know if I had what it took to be that confident. Minutes later I found my answer, it was a dirty blond-haired man's fearlessness.

The neighborhood was unlike any I'd ever seen. It had beautiful hundred-year-old Victorian homes and the gay men who saw the beauty behind their crumbling facades were bringing them back to life in stunning ways. I felt I'd gone through the looking glass; nothing in San Francisco resembled anything I knew in Wisconsin. Unlike cold hard Wisconsin, everything here was alive and saturated with beauty.

Kerry's address was a white, three-story Victorian, and I carefully scanned the names and apartment numbers in the directory next to the front door. My chest was pounding with a tsunami of joy as I rang Kerry's brass apartment button.

"Yes?" came his scratchy voice. "Who is it?"

"Your cousin Paul. C'mon, buzz me in."

"Paul!" he shrieked. "You made it! Come on up. My door is to your left at the second-floor landing."

When I got there, he opened the door in harem pants and sandals. "Look at you!" he said.

I smiled. "I'm growing my hair long like the hippies."

"Come in. Grab a seat."

"I can't believe there are so many good-looking men," I said as I entered the incense-infused room.

"I'm just getting used to it. Everyone one here is so free and everything's going our way. This is our time!"

I noticed Kerry was more toned and fit. "You're better looking than the last time I saw you."

"The big difference is I came out and made peace with myself."

"Is it true I can actually be anyone I want to be?"

"You can be a dumbass fool if you want."

I put my duffle bag next to the door and sat on a sofa. "I don't know where to start."

"If I know you, you want sex. And if that's what you want, just go out and start meeting guys."

"So, I just walk up and introduce myself?"

"With your looks that won't be difficult. The city is astonishing but it takes a little getting used to. Madison wasn't like this, that's for sure."

"You have to show me around."

"Social life here is mostly the bars, and parties stop at eleven."

"San Francisco has a law prohibiting late parties?"

"It might as well have. You can set your clock by it. I've never been to a party that lasted much past ten forty-five, when everyone heads to the bars. There's nothing like San Francisco. I keep surprising myself with the men I bring home. A warning; you always have to be the best at whatever you do but here that won't be easy. When you start dating there are a lot of talented men you'll be up against."

"I'd be grateful for anyone who knows there's more to sex than fumbling around on a daybed."

"Here, let me give you a quick tour." He spread a map on the coffee table and pointed as he moved around the map. "The bars on Polk Street up there are full of twinks and Cher fanatics. You want to go to Castro Street. Bars over there are popping up like mushrooms and Toad Hall is my favorite and I could stare at Michael behind the bar all day. If you get interested in kink and I know you will, the leather bars are on Folsom Street south of Market. If you don't like bars, there's a bunch of bathhouses."

"Huh? You mean like gymnasiums?"

"No, they're complete paradise and the safest place in town for a gay man. Tuesdays are two-for-one, so I go with friends. I've never had a bad time at the baths. It doesn't get any better and that's why this is our time. Gay men don't hide their sex in the closet; they tell everyone they're proud of it."

"I never thought I'd ever find a place like this."

"My advice, get out there and meet as many as you can, and if you like a guy I'm sure he's willing to have more of you."

I never thought of myself as good looking, but at those cocktail parties I knew I had something gay men wanted. Kerry was saying gay men in San Francisco would also want it, but here the stakes were higher. "So, I should meet one man after the next?" This was beyond my wildest imaginings.

"It's the best way to make friends. You meet someone, you sleep with him, and then you're friends."

"So, you're saying I can walk out the door, find the bar and get back here with a man before midnight?"

"You'd be having sex in fifteen minutes but not here because I'd want in on the action."

"Can we go to the bars tonight?" I couldn't wait to see my first gay bar.

"Before we go, there are things you should know. Men are going to look at you, they will cruise you, which is the way we check each other out. The first time a man cruised me, I freaked; I felt exposed. You're a good-looking man, so men are going to cruise you, and you need be able to handle it. It's an art, but knowing *you*, it won't take you long to figure it out."

"But how do I start a conversation?"

"We're all strangers and the men in the bars are just as scared as you are. Asking them where they're from is a good way to start a conversation and sharing coming out stories is pretty common; that's how I learned how to be gay. Once you start meeting guys you'll find your style but don't overdo it."

"There's so much to learn."

"Once I've played with someone it's easy. I start by catching up on what he's doing. I might comment on something stupid a politician said and then we smoke a joint. I already know what he likes to do so I try to make it as much fun for him as it is for me."

"It's really that easy?"

"I'm going country and western dancing with friends tonight. You want to join us?"

"You in your harem pants bought into that he-man John Wayne cowboy bullshit. What the fuck?"

"I have a ball every time we go."

"If I may, what about your sex life?"

He smiled. "I do quite well, thank you very much. Don't have a boyfriend, but I'm seeing someone and I have a date tonight, so you are on your own and your only problem is deciding which bar you want to go to."

I laughed and shook my head. "The idea of a bar for just gay men still gets me."

"There were fifty-five last count."

"Holy shit!"

Kerry checked his watch. "I gotta run out and get things for dinner. You wanna come with me?"

I pulled a book from my duffle bag. "I don't need to see another supermarket."

He stood. "There's something else you need to know. Food in San Francisco is almost as sacred as sex. If you're gonna make it here, you're gonna have to make a decent omelet. I try to cook something new at my dinner parties. Don't be scared. Cooking's lot of fun."

"But you waddled around your mother every time she made a meal."

"I beg your pardon. I hardly waddled."

"But you watched her every move."

"The other thing you should know is that men here want to change the world."

I scoffed. "I didn't come here to be a lab rat."

"You've been a rebel ever since you moved the Bible to the fiction section in the library."

Moving to San Francisco I wasn't just changing geography, I was changing the way I saw myself as a man. Back home I didn't see the limits because I took them for granted, but uptight Wisconsin limited almost every aspect of my life. Now without limits I was forging an identity and to make it as an out gay man I had to trust my instincts.

The following morning I left Kerry's ready to make friends, but the nearest bar had only a smattering of patrons so I stopped for an early lunch at a café on Castro Street. I sat on the metal chair at a table in the window and a handsome man cruised me. I wanted to meet him but I didn't know how to cruise him back and that sent me into a momentary downer. I was pouting when a man with a red beard at the next table leaned over. "You're new, aren't you?"

I smiled, embarrassed. "I just got here. Is everyone here out?"

"It's a real coming together of out gay men. I'd be happy to show you around. My name is Scott. I've got to get back to work, but can you meet me tonight at seven and we can start at my favorite Toad Hall."

I shook his hand. "I'm Paul and thank you so much. I'll be there."

The bar was shoulder to shoulder men and by the time we got to the bar to order drinks, Scott and I were wedged between men in flannel shirts and jeans. The men around us had beards and many of them had beautiful shoulder length hair. I wanted to become one of them more than I'd wanted anything.

"You're getting a lot of attention so I'm going to wander around." He started walking away.

"Is there a guidebook?" I grabbed his arm.

"Oh, you mean for tourists?"

"No, a book that teaches me how to enjoy sex."

Scott grinned. "That's so sweet. You're the first man I've met who's so upfront. The truth of the matter is, the best way to learn how to enjoy sex is to just do it, and you're not going to have any trouble finding someone who'll jump into bed with you."

The handsome bartender smiled at me and nodded.

Scott saw me looking. "Be careful you don't fall in love. Michael's a special kind of guy.

"Don't worry. I'm not the kind who falls in love."

"I'll hate you if you make a date with him before I do," he joked and slipped into the crowd.

I asked Michael for another beer and I was instantly taken by his curly black hair and his thick arm as he pulled a bottle from the sweating cooler. He put the bottle on a coaster in front of me and when I looked up expecting to meet his gaze but he was already on his way down the bar to a customer waving an empty glass. I wasn't going to let this stop me from meeting Michael some other time.

I went outside for a smoke, and after the sweltering bar, the cool night air was refreshing. Scott was outside, doing the same. I said, "It feels like I'm dreaming."

He smiled. "There's never been anything like this."

"I wonder what our gay ancestors would have thought of what we're doing. It makes me want to know who they were."

"You mean the gay men who came before us?"

"Yes. If I knew what life was like for them, I might have a better understanding of how I got to where I am as a gay man."

"The main library might have what you're looking for and the first-floor men's room is hot and I mean hot."

"You mean?"

He nodded.

"Thanks. I'll check it out."

The library's Beaux Arts foyer and imposing staircase lent an air of adventure to my search but before I began my quest, I slipped into the men's room where a towhead in jeans was more than happy to give me a blow job. He surprised me when he said, "Thank you," when he finished blowing me.

Back in search mode, I walked to the information desk and asked the woman in a blue work shirt and cropped hair, "Can you direct me to books about men?"

"The best place to start is the card catalog over there." I didn't know what lesbians looked like but she acted like she knew what I wanted.

I scanned the bank of drawers in the blond wood catalog that was as old as the building and pulled out the first H drawer expecting to find cards for books about homosexuality. I found titles about ancient Greek and Roman cultures that I knew, as well as a couple of medical books, but nothing about my living gay brothers and sisters. Where were our novels, biographies, memoirs and histories? I then turned to an S drawer for 'sex', thinking there had to be something there. Based what I'd seen, if there was a category gay men owned it was sex. What I found as I fingered through the cards were clinical sounding titles. How could the main library of a city that embraced sexual liberation have no books about its gay people? I was disappointed but I didn't want to leave the library without learning something, so to prepare myself for sex with the men who'd teach me how to enjoy sex, I went back to the medical books and examined the full color drawings of the inside of a penis and testicles and the maze of colons that end in an ass.

I left through the main reading room and the title

City of Night caught my eye. It suggested it was the book I'd been looking for, so I eagerly opened it to a page of drag queens. That wasn't what I expected but gay men were in print on the page and I shivered with excitement as I read the next page about a dismal city of hustler sex and it a sleazy encounter. I couldn't believe such a book existed! In a public library! I walked out of the library elated; I'd found a gay ancestor! As I crossed Civic Center plaza I couldn't understand why the city didn't have more useful information for men like me who were coming out. I decided to build a collection on my own and use *City of Night* as its foundation so gay men and lesbians struggling with their sexuality had honest information.

I had no experience finding books, and it wasn't going to be easy or happen overnight, but a collection was my way of thanking the city for letting me be myself.

TWO

I began collecting in earnest the next day by stopping by Paperback Traffic, a well-lit book store on Castro Street that I'd seen gay men going in and out of all day. The beat writers were legends and I took my copy of *Howl* out of my pack and leaned against the wall. When I looked up an older man was cruising me. I still hadn't figured out how to cruise so I smiled politely and turned away. Later, as I was trying to get my head around Allen Ginsberg's genius, I felt a tap on my shoulder, and when I turned it was the older man.

"Can you spare a minute?" he asked. "I saw you in Dolores Park and it looked like you're here for a reason."

"What can I do for you?" His freckled face and his curiosity intrigued me.

"When I was your age I'd just come out and I'd be summarily fired if my boss found out I was a gay. If my landlord saw anything even vaguely homo in my mail, my possessions would be tossed on the street and the locks would be changed. The only time I could be seen with other men was after dark in out of the way places. Would you be so kind as to let me watch you live the way I couldn't?"

"That must have been ugly, and by the way, my name in Paul. I just got here." I reached for his hand.

He gripped my hand. "I'm sorry. I should have introduced myself. Mom couldn't decide on a name and settled on Fletcher Edward Arthur Gillibrand but please call me Eddie. I grew up on a ranch in Sonoma County."

"Are you rich?" I was curious because he was impeccably dressed.

"When San Francisco was rebuilding from the earthquake in 1906 the demand for timber skyrocketed. My grandfather's limber business made a fortune decimating vast tracts of redwoods and I live with the shame of what he did."

"But you must have grown up with everything."

"I did but the one thing that was missing was love."

"And now you're trying to make up for that?"

"It's selfish, but I want to watch you as you became the gay San Franciscan I couldn't be. I know people in high places and I may be able to help you on your journey."

"You'd do that? What was it like in your day?"

"It wasn't like it is today. We had to use ways to identify each other. Pinky rings and saying you're a friend of Dorothy were clues that a man was gay. There were only a few bars and if I saw a man in one of them one night I couldn't acknowledge him if I saw him on the street the next day. I can't describe the hurt I felt when the man who's whispered 'You're the man I've been looking for' acts like I'm evil incarnate and avoids looking at me next day. Just going to a gay bar was risky because we never knew if the cops were going to raid it, especially as it got closer to elections. The day after a raid a complete list of the full names of all the men who'd been arrested would be published in the *Chronicle,* so everyone in town knew you were a homo. Living with secrecy fucks with your mind. Every time I stepped out of my apartment I had to keep track of two personalities and I might have to switch between them several times in an hour. I didn't know who I could trust and I had to run everything I was about to say through elaborate plumbing to make sure that what came out of my mouth didn't give me away. I'd say something umpteen different ways to myself to make sure that what I said out loud sounded just like what my straight coworker would say. We bought into the culture around us. Can you imagine how hard it is to love yourself when you can't acknowledge who you are? I was a ghost with my family and kinda to me, too. It shouldn't surprise you that men, including me, turned to booze to ease the pain. It was a daily pain and a constant reminder that I wasn't worthy; I was the scum of the earth and shouldn't be permitted to live. I was lucky because I had something inside that whispered, "You're gonna make it," and an innate hope that things would get better. Some sad souls who couldn't take it gave up hope and jumped off the bridge. Anyone who's lived that kind of life has the authority to say 'fuck you' to anyone who says, "You chose to be gay.'"

"I know this might sound strange but how's that going to affect me?"

"That's a perfectly normal question and I'd like to be your friend so I can help you as you go through your coming out."

That was a lot to take in and he didn't answer my question so I didn't know what to say. "You'd be looking over my shoulder."

"I promise you won't notice. Your generation is going through a transformation in the way they think about sex that boggles my mind. Being gay in San Francisco is entirely different than it was five years ago, and I don't want you to miss that. My friends Bill and Jim are experimenting with what they call pleasuring."

This was just what I wanted. "Sure, but would they like me?"

"I know they would; I can already tell you're a perfect match to the new kind of thinking."

"How do you know that?"

"Paul, if you pardon my French, you're a mound of oozing sexuality. I know you're going to protest, but face it, you're what they call hot and no one's going to stop you if you want to get out there and take advantage of it. Would you like to meet them?"

"Yes, can you tell? I asked looking down at my tented pants.

"Growing up we're taught sex is a nasty business, but when you stop and think about it, sex is a natural urge and it doesn't matter with whom you do it."

"I should have been home an hour ago."

Eddie took my hand. "I'm sorry if I overdid it. You should go. Think about it. Your life is going to be so grand."

"Will you give me your number?" He gave me his phone number and said, "I'll tell Bill and Jim we met."

On dark winter nights in Wisconsin I felt there had to be a way I could be a sane gay man and now with the prospect of meeting Bill and Jim there was a chance I'd learn how.

The next day I saw a man with a trim red-brown beard and chiseled features hauling groceries from his car, and I was beginning to think every spectacular beauty in the country lived in San Francisco. He looked up and smiled. "Did I see you the other night at Toad Hall?" he asked.

"I was the one at the end of the bar."

"I'm Clay. You looked lost. Are you new in town?" His smile was warm.

"I'm Paul and I got here a couple days ago. Yesterday a really nice man helped me find a place."

"I suppose it would be silly to ask if you're here for the bridges. I'm surprised every day by the number of men who show up."

"Then I'm one of the lucky ones."

"I think your name was on the special guest list." He grinned.

"You're not the first person who said something like that. I don't get it. I'm just a kid from the Midwest."

"I've been here long enough to know that some men get by on their looks, but you have something strong going on inside. You're here to prove something."

"If anything, I'd like to know that even though I love sex, I'm sane."

"You've come to just the right place at just the right time. The stars are aligned."

"You're just saying that."

"Would you like to come to my place tonight around seven? I'll prove I'm not just saying that. Here's my number."

I had a raging erection and scribbled his address on

a scrap of paper. I folded it neatly and slipped into my wallet.

He said, "I'll leave the door ajar."

That afternoon at my kitchen table I was certain our encounter was a fluke. If I went to Clay's, he wouldn't be there. I was asking too much to think a man as good looking as Clay was interested in me. I'd never been so nervous and decided to save the embarrassment and stay home, but in the shower, I thought about being the center of his attention and I had never been the center of anyone's attention. As I toweled off I decided to go to Clay's, find him gone and turn the rejection into a funny anecdote about being stood up by a hot man. How many guys could say that? Besides, if I was going to survive in a city of men who had sex whenever they wanted to, I had better get used to rejection. I felt better when I told myself this one rejection wasn't going to stop me from following Kerry's lead and go home with as many men as I could.

I stopped at the top of the path to his home. My date with Clay was the most important thing I'd ever done. When I saw him in the bar he was surrounded by a group of the most excited men I'd ever seen and he was the handsomest man in a group of handsome men. I couldn't stop thinking of having sex with Clay who'd know interesting ways of having sex I hadn't thought of, and learning how to enjoy sex was why I'd come to San Francisco. I was putting my life as a gay man on the line with Clay. I wanted him to want me, but I didn't know how to seduce men. I wanted Clay to touch me the way he touched the men in the bar, a touch that meant something—the touch I longed for growing up but I never got. I wanted to be swept off my feet but I really didn't know what swept meant because the only sweeping I wanted with the man in Wisconsin was to sweep him out the door.

This was my new life as a gay man and I wanted to end my date with Clay a winner. If I fell in love with him, would I know it? With Mother still grieving Father's death, there was no room for love at home, so I wouldn't know love if it slapped me in the face. Clay was handsome but he wanted to know me and nobody ever cared about me.

I wanted Clay to think I was worthy of being his boyfriend and that was asking a lot. I couldn't think of a more exciting life than being his boyfriend. It was the kind of life I dreamed of where we would go out to dinner together, go to movies together and make love at night and in the morning and whenever we felt like having sex. If people saw me with Clay, they would think I was worth knowing and his handsome friends would become my friends. For someone like me who'd never had many friends, that was huge.

Clay's door was ajar so I pushed it open and peeked in. He saw me and said, "You OK? There's no bear inside. Come in. Come in. Can I get you something to drink?"

"I'd love some wine," I said as I crossed the threshold.

"I hope red's good. I should have asked." He stumbled when he hugged me.

"It's fine." If Clay had served Kool-Aid I would have been eternally grateful.

Clay went to the kitchen and returned with a bottle of wine and two glasses.

"Tell me about what it was like growing up? Did you have a best friend you played hide and seek with? Were your parents good to you?"

I took a glass. "Father died when I was ten, and Mother is still dealing with it and not very well."

"I'm so sorry. So, you didn't have a happy childhood?"

"I spent a lot of time in the library and fell in love with books."

"What are your favorites? Have you read Gore Vidal? He's a scream."

"I don't know this Vidal guy."

"He's probably one of the smartest writers alive and he makes sure you know it. His *Myra Breckenridge* is about a man who undergoes a sex change. When I started reading it, I thought Vidal was a lunatic, but when I finished reading it I thought the rest of the world was full of lunatics."

"I want to read it and add it to my collection."

"You have a collection? That's so cool. Nobody reads these days."

"My collection will have honest books about sex and sexuality so kids who are coming to grips with their sexuality will have books to help make it easier."

"Our work is never done and your collection is just what we need."

"If you want me to do political work I'm really not cut out for that."

"One day we think we've made a lot of progress and the next day it's taken away. We're ahead of the rest of the country but that's no excuse to sit back. Our struggle is a long one, and that's why it's so important for us to come out to our parents. Your collection fits right in. If parents know a gay person it's harder for them to hate gay people. If an out gay person is sitting across the table from a bigot, his mere presence changes the conversation."

"I thought everything here was going to be easy."

"We'll get to the sex part later. I've got to finish in in the kitchen. Hold on." He went back to the kitchen. While he was gone, I looked around Clay's living room that was filled with art and tchotchkes. My head was full of decorating ideas inspired by what I saw when Clay served dinner. I'd never eaten a meal sitting on the floor, and I got a perverse pleasure eating his Indian lamb dish with my hands. Feeling very full, I wiped my hands on the napkin in my lap.

"Let's wash up and smoke a joint," Clay said.

I didn't tell him I'd never smoked weed. "Sure, that's fine with me."

When I smoked, I coughed but that didn't faze him. "Gay life here is even better than I expected. I've been to Toad Hall and saw the bartender Michael. There's something about him."

"He's a one of a kind."

"My cousin said there were all these gay bath houses. Are there really that many?"

"You have a lot to choose from. One just opened with a roof that opens to the sky. Ritch Street was the first of the big baths designed by a gay man for gay men. It has a sauna, a steam room maze, and two floors of cubicles with thin mattress not much larger than a man to lie on. The sleazier ones south of Market don't pretend to be baths; they are just rooms and most of them have gang showers and one has a toilet with a hose for cleaning out, but I'm going too fast. I'll save that for when you've been here awhile."

"No, please. I know it sounds weird, but I want to know how men here have sex. What's cleaning out?"

"If you're going to get fucked, you want your ass clean. I use the hose in my shower for that."

"Does it feel good?" I didn't mention I was shocked.

"The warm water is very comforting but it takes a little getting used to."

"I could get used to that." I was surprised I said that.

"You're really here for the sex, aren't you?"

"I spent years dreaming I would someday be a full blown gay man and now I'm here and I've just scratched the surface."

"The city's the proverbial candy store, and you have a lot of candy to choose from."

"I know this sounds stupid, but are they all the same?"

"I think of it as three shelves of candy. The top row is kissing and cuddling, the next level is oral sex, sucking cock and the third is anal sex."

"I'm not sure I like the idea of having something in my ass."

"That's exactly what I thought. It runs counter to nature. Our asses are designed to hold things in, but when you're being fucked, you reverse the order and since our asses are lined with thousands of receptors the feeling is spectacular."

"Really?"

"Believe me, it'll be a shock at first, but you are going to love it. You will like it so much, you'll have to learn how to not get carried away."

"Now you're talking crazy."

"Paul, anal sex drives this city. If you're going to make it, you better get comfortable with having something in your ass and some even go beyond dicks."

"Don't a lot of guys use drugs?"

"Most men use poppers when they fuck but the

men I know usually just smoke weed." He got up and refilled my wine glass.

"Do you know Bill and Jim?" I asked. "I'd like to meet them."

"You must have met Eddie."

"You know Eddie?"

"Eddie helps guys like you get settled. You can't meet a nicer guy and I also know Bill and Jim. They taught me how to create and receive pleasure."

"What's this pleasure thing? Anything fun was considered a sin back home."

"They can talk to you about sex better than I can."

"Really? I've always wanted to talk about sex but I had no one who'd talk about it."

"You've come to the right place."

"I'm really excited to get into all kinds of sex. Can I say that?"

"Of course you can, but take your time. Don't have sex just to put notches on your belt. Sex is an art that should be savored with a friend. Some guys like one-time sex but I like knowing the men I have sex with. I have regular buddies, and my sex with them is always the best."

"Let me get this straight, you have sex partners but you're not lovers?"

"This is the Age of Aquarius, and we can do anything we want, as long as it feels good. You are here at a magical time, Paul. Bill and Jim are showing men they don't have to be scared of sex, instead, they should revel in it and spread the joy around."

"That sounds crazy to me."

"It is crazy but crazy good. Let me show you a few crazy things in the bedroom."

His bedroom looked like an Arabian tent. I was caught off guard when he began to undress and I scrambled to undress, and as I did I watched closely, so I'd know what to do when I started a future date. Clay lit a joint and with a gentle nudge pushed me onto the waterbed. He slid his hand under the top of my underpants, which he slipped them past my feet and tossed them over his shoulder with a single swipe. I was shivering with excitement when he lay on top of me. Feeling him there was the most rewarding kind of comfort; I was part of Clay. When we kissed with our tongues, I was mesmerized by this man of staggering good looks and I had to wrap my legs around him and nuzzle his chest. With my head full of his musk, I was a giant and I was hard as a rock. I wanted to hold him and never let go. I shuddered when I felt the tip of his spit-lubricated dick pressed against my hole. I took a deep breath as his long slender dick slipped slowly inside me, my attention shifted from my head to my hole. The feeling was completely new and it took me a few minutes to adjust to having him inside me.

"Just relax." He began running his tongue around my ear.

As I rocked languidly with him inside me I closed my eyes and the longer he stayed inside me the warmer I felt. I didn't expect I would be so willing to let a man fuck me, and without intending my body took charge and I began to relax. As he continued slowly fucking me I began to merge with his body, and I had nothing to compare to the serenity I was feeling. When he noticed I'd relaxed a bit, he picked up the pace. When I looked at his face it was a face completely free of wrinkles. When our eyes connected bolts of electricity shot fire from my head to my toes, it was as if I'd just been waiting to be fucked and I wanted to smother him in kisses. My ass burned and I pushed back to get more of him. With my legs, around him, he turned us so we were side by side and his prick slid against a different part of my ass and that was even more exciting. I yelled, "Fuck me!!"

Clay slowed down and took me to a space of supreme happiness where I wanted to dive inside of him. I couldn't get enough of him. My head was on a distant planet when my insides began to rumble and my head threw back as my climax filled my navel with knots of ivory-colored jism. "Oh, my god!"

"Thank you! You have an amazing ass and you handled it like a pro."

"Thank you!"

We smoked a joint in the kitchen, and he said, "I want to spend more time with you. Would you be interested in camping?"

"I've never been outside the city."

"What a shame. Then you are in for a real treat. I'd like to spend a weekend with you in a sacred redwood forest and we are going to do mushrooms if you think you're ready for them."

"Thanks. That sounds great." I had never been more ready.

"The mushrooms are mind-alerting hallucinogens. They are an amazing drug that opens me to a world inside me I didn't know existed."

"I can't think of a better of way of trying them than with you."

"I know you're going to have an amazing trip."

I was a different man when I walked home. Layers of barriers had been stripped away and I was naked. But I wasn't scared. It was like coming out again and the first time I could call myself a man. In the cool night air I was Paul Bullen, expertly-fucked gay man and proud of it.

THREE

I couldn't wait to see Clay again and he was walking on his toes when he met me at the door. "I can't wait to get started. How did you find the forest?" Clay had an aura that intrigued me and I wanted to get into his head.

"I spent a couple weeks there last summer with a band of healers who lived there all summer and only went into town for food."

"So, it's in a wilderness area."

"The only way to know its beauty is to be there and I know you're going to love it."

I got into his beat-up Karman Ghia and Clay got behind the wheel. We crossed the Golden Gate Bridge clouded in fog and drove through the tunnel. Granite outcroppings around the tunnel gave way to the lowlands of the Bay marshes and their flocks of waterfowl. The forests and grasslands of Marin were interrupted by the small towns and traffic slowed as people got on and off the freeway. When we crossed into Sonoma County the landscape changed to gentler hills of brown grass and grazing herds of black and white cattle. A farmer on a tractor dragged a steel harrow across an uneven field. Further into the county vineyards began appearing with their regular rows of staked clumps of grapes and crumbled dry ground and workers bent over harvesting the first grapes of the year. Further on fat oaks with wild arms gave way to towering redwood sentries. After passing several rows of them Clay turned off 101 and took us down a single lane road that cut through a redwood forest. We'd been traveling on it for some time when we crossed a concrete bridge. On the other side of the bridge Clay pulled the gravel side of the road and stopped. I wanted it to be the perfect weekend for both of us, and my greatest fear was disappointing Clay. He got out without opening the door and I got out and helped him unload provisions. Before I could hike my pack, Clay unbuttoned his flannel shirt and pulled it off his shoulders and sun caught the red hairs on his chest. He opened the top of his 501s, loosened the buttons and let them drop to the dirt. When he bent over to loosen his boots I saw his perfect ass. My eyes stayed glued to him as he leaned on the rusting fender to remove his thick cotton socks and flapped to dry them before stashing them behind the driver's seat. It was my turn to undress and I did my best to make it as erotic as he'd made his and I didn't try to hide my erection. We stood naked face to face and he bent into me and slipped his tongue in my mouth. "Welcome to magic. Follow me." As I walked behind him as we traversed the pebbled creek bed. We passed a clump of willows and I wanted him to push me onto them and lick my face. Just as I was about the put my foot into a thicket of them he screamed, "Avoid the nettles!" When I reached a convergence of two streams I was coasted with a fine layer of glistening sweat. I stepped onto a mound of grass and Clay told me, "Take three steps and turn around." I took them and when I turned I was standing in the middle of a ring of giant redwoods. I didn't realize how immense the majestic monsters were until I looked up and they kept going, leaving little room for the sun.

Standing naked and surrounded by giants I knew why this place was sacred. The trees were a cathedral to the earth mother Goddess, the bearer of life and witness to the generosity of nature. Clay saw me standing in awe. "It's called a faerie ring. Pretty incredible, isn't it?" he said.

I was humbled as I unloaded my pack on a platform cut from a fallen redwood. Clay rebuilt a stone fire ring and he yelled, "Hang the food high so the raccoons wouldn't get it." I strung a backpack with our food in a tree and joined Clay on the grass and dangled my feet in the creek as tiny fish competed against the flow of the creek as they swam upstream. Clay passed a joint and I said, "These trees are so tall and so old!" I sensed the magic of the place and closed my eyes to take it in.

"Eddie said you're collecting books." Clay splashed water across my legs.

"I want to find my gay ancestors."

He wrapped me in his arms and we slid onto the creek's sandy bottom. "I think I like you."

"I like you, too."

Under a blazing sun, I remained barefoot as we splashed upstream through thick clumps of yellowing willow. The skin on my shoulders was beginning to glow when Clay pulled a limb off a tree, struck a fencing pose and yelled, "En garde!" I scrambled to find a limb, broke it off and struck the same pose. We did mock battle like a couple of schoolboys until he wrapped me in his arms and again I was helpless to fend off his kisses. After much kissing and being close I was on my back and without saying a word Clay let me know he was about to enter me. This time I knew what to expect and I wanted him. With just a soft moan, he slipped inside me and my world turned backwards and upside down and I floated high above the creek. I begged for more and wondered how I could return his joy. Having him inside me was the most gratifying feeling I'd ever known, an ecstasy that words diminish. Clay and I were brothers and lovers; we were an orbiting planet and we were the sun. I'd never felt that close to another man; I was no longer just me, I was part of Paul and Clay. As the happiest man on earth, the only thing that mattered was Clay. I didn't want the warm feelings to end but eventually after many minutes of profound connection I couldn't stop my cock with a mind of its own and it sent shock waves down my spine and up my cock and I climaxed!

I glowed when I rinsed off in the creek and Clay glowed when he stepped out of the woods like a Norse god. He said, "Grab some fallen branches." I didn't want to be away from him but I shuffled off in search of brush and came back with an armful of broken limbs. I snuggled next to him around the fire and touching him again filled me with joy. We sat bum to bum exchanging energies in silence until the sun was just an orange sliver on the horizon.

Clay whispered, "You're a beautiful man." When he said that, I started to cry. He took me in his arms. "I knew I was going to like you when I saw you on the street. Sometimes the universe provides."

"You are very special." What I felt for Clay was an extraordinary feeling that made me stop and think, is this love? Is this happening to me? The urge to let loose and tell him I loved him was fierce but something held me back.

"What's going on? A minute ago, you were light as

a feather and now you look like your dog got run over by a semi."

"I'm afraid to love." My words surprised me.

He took my hand. "Emotions are tricky, but when I feel something I go with it. You're a very special man, Paul. You may not think that but you are."

"But I do."

"In the Age of Aquarius words don't matter, feelings do."

"I've never felt these feelings. They're out of control."

"Being out of control is a wonderful place to be."

"This isn't like what I see in movies. It comes from deep inside."

"Love is raw and sometimes it hurts. I feel very close to you." His breath on my neck got me hard. He pulled his knees against my butt and we lay listening to our breathing. Time passed and as I moved just enough to feel him against me, I saw us crossing a field of freshly mown grass, then we were floating with the current. As long as he was with me I was content. I fought back the urge to have sex and the longer we stayed there without it, the closer I felt to him. I'm not sure who started, but we began making love that lifted me and making love in a redwood cathedral took me higher. He started as the leader but as we played he let me take the lead. I noticed which gestures of mine that turned him on and kept going back to them and our play became a gentle contest of me giving Clay as much joy as he gave me and vice versa. After much rolling around and kissing, we came almost simultaneously. I was floating when I kissed and him. "Thank you." So much had happened I had to lie on a patch of grass in late morning sun to take it all in. Finally, I found the energy to say, "I would never have found this magic."

"Don't move. I'm going to get the mushrooms."

"Can hallucinogens make *this* any better?"

He pulled a deep purple velvet pouch from his pack and extracted shrivel bits of mushrooms and laid them on a rock. "I'm letting them absorb the sun's energy."

I went to the creek and rinsed off and when I came back Clay put a scrap of mushroom on my tongue. "It'll take twenty minutes and if you get scared yell." With a wet finger, he took a scrap of mushroom to his tongue, bowed to the sun, and wandered downstream leaving me alone. I didn't know what would happen, but knowing Clay would never be far gave me confidence to slosh my way upstream. I stopped at a bend in the creek where a fallen log made a mossy waterfall. I squatted in the creek and my feet attracted minnows that nibbled on the peeling skin of my toes. I plucked a handful of pebbles from the shallows and traded them from hand to hand and decided the perfectly round white stone and dark stone of gnarled quartz veined with red were my two halves. The white one was my rational self and the gnarled quartz was my sexual self. I traded them again several times and found no resolve so I tossed them in the stream and realized I was both halves. I splashed back to our camp, took my journal from my backpack and returned the creek. I sat next to a pool in the stream and put my favorite pen to a fresh journal page but instead of writing the pen made squiggles that looked like the doodling of a lunatic. I was stoned!!!

I was naked to the world and I was the other Paul I'd never seen who'd been under my skin since the day I was born. This man I'd never known was looking back at me in in the reflection in the pool, and I wasn't afraid of him. He was the Paul who had the guts to drop out of college to follow a dream, the Paul who wanted to experience life in all its warts and promises. I stood and water fell slipping from me. I started walking and Father's face morphed from the lopsided crown of a redwood in approval. In a world that made sense to me in a new way, water flew from my feet as I splashed downstream in search of Clay. I was laughing when I found him in the lotus position atop a fallen log. He was peaceful so I moved silently, but he heard me laughing. "Having fun?"

"The mushrooms *are* magic. I never saw all of me before."

"You are the reflections in a prism and you are the prism. Did I just say that? I haven't been this stoned since I did mushrooms with a healer last year."

"I saw Father in a tree and he was proud of me."

"Is he dead? I'm so sorry."

"He died when I was ten."

"That has to be hard for you."

"I tried not to think of him, but he's with me every day."

"He meant a lot to you."

"On his last day, he said I should follow my heart."

"I know it's sad, but he had to be one of the best fathers of all time to say that."

"I have picture taken the year before he died, and I look like him."

"That's why he's with you all the time. He wanted to you lead this life."

"You think?"

"He loved you and he would want you to be happy. That's what good dads want for their kids. Are you happy?"

"I was pretty fucked up until I moved here, and if I may say so, being with you makes me extremely happy."

"Do I qualify for member of your family?"

"Let me think about that." I paused long enough for him to think I meant it and then said, "You're fucking right! You're not just a member of my family, you *are* my family."

"That deserves a kiss."

FOUR

I didn't recognize the window. My bedroom didn't have metal windows, and it wasn't my room and it was so white it hurt my eyes. I reached for my throbbing head and felt a bandage. I was scared.

"I'm glad you're alive." The voice sounded like it came through a tunnel.

When I tried to speak, I had trouble moving my lips. "Who's that?"

"It's Clay and I didn't think you were going to make it."

"What am I doing here?"

"You're in the hospital and your speech is slurred."

"What's this on my head? I don't like it."

"You've been here three days. When you got here they did surgery on your head and you need to rest."

"Am I going to die?"

He pulled a chair next to my bed and put his head next to mine. "You're going to be fine. Let me start at the beginning. Three days ago, I heard a thud on my door. When I got there, you were curled up in a ball and when I tapped your shoulder you said you had a headache and asked me for an aspirin. I don't know how you made it in your condition but I knew something was wrong and called my doctor. When I described your condition, he told me to get you to the hospital immediately so he could X-ray your head. You mumbled something to him about kids yelling 'not in our neighborhood.' The doctor could tell you'd been hit on the head by a blunt instrument but there was no bleeding. He did the X-rays anyway and they showed four places where your skull was fractured and there was also a pool of blood on your brain."

"Blood on my brain. That's scary." I touched my head and it hurt so I pulled back.

"You're going to be fine. Once you were out of surgery my doctor asked you what happened and you muttered something about not moving because you didn't want to get hit again."

"The last thing I remember is going out to look for books."

"Somewhere you were mugged. They did the surgery on your skull because you had what they call a subdural hematoma. That's like a blood clot and they had to drill a hole in your head in relieve the pressure on your brain."

"I hope they missed my brain."

"Glad you still have your sense of humor."

"I've gotta rest. I really do."

The next thing I knew it was dark outside. I heard, "I came to see how you were doing."

I had trouble focusing on the voice. "Who's there?"

"It's Eddie and Clay's here, too. I was horrified when Clay told me what happened to you."

"You didn't have to come," I slurred.

"Tragedies like this have to stop. I won't put up with it," Eddie said.

"Eddie he's going to cover your hospital bills."

"Can someone get me some water?" So much had happened and my brain wasn't fully functioning and all I wanted was rest.

Clay poured water into the paper cup on the tray and handed it to me.

"I didn't think this was going to happen but your collection is upsetting neighbors and you need to stop collecting for a while," Eddie said.

"I can't believe you're saying that. You've been the one talking up Paul's collection," Clay said.

"Longtime residents don't like the gentrification that's going on in the Castro. If we are ever going to get our rights, we can't do it all right now, we have to respect their feelings and go from there. A collection is a great step forward, but the rest of the city isn't ready for a gay collection at this moment."

I mustered the energy and asked, "I'm not going to let a little bop on my head stop me from collecting."

"But why not stop for a year or two?" Eddie asked.

"Eddie, he needs to rest and I gotta run." Clay kissed me on the cheek and left.

Two weeks later I was having dinner at Eddie's and my arm went numb. I shook it, but it stayed numb and then my hand started twitching and after that, I tumbled to the floor with my arms and legs flailing. I was conscious and lay there some time. Eddie helped me get up.

"You had a seizure. Have your doctor get you a prescription."

"I'm so embarrassed."

"Nothing to be embarrassed about. My cousin has them."

I got a prescription, and a week after that I was home and my arm went numb again. I knew what was coming and lay on the floor and let the seizure run its course. I didn't tell anyone because I didn't want them to worry and I got a second prescription.

My world had changed. The chance I could fall

remained in the back of my mind and I treated each day as precious. Every time I entered a space I looked for places to curl up if my arm went dumb. The city was more precious, too. I took the Castro for granted, but now I needed its support more than ever. It felt strange to love a city, but I loved San Francisco. It was not just its freedom that let me be me but it was a feeling that everyone in the city mattered and we were a family. Friends became more important. My good looks had a shelf-life and I didn't think the seizures would make me flawed merchandise, but I could no longer take for granted that men would come home with me. Friendships that started with sex now needed to be nurtured.

I was getting depressed, and when I was down, I went to one of the city's cobbled together neighborhoods and watched my fellow San Franciscans go about their lives. A young Japanese-American woman helping her son climb to the top of the slide gave me hope for the future. Seeing the murals of early California on walls in the Mission reminded me that I was not the only stranger who came here to live free. Eating dim sum in a Chinatown restaurant surrounded by children, even though they drove me crazy, reminded me that immigrant groups like mine were thriving. I started exploring the city's past and found the address but not the building where Gertrude Stein grew up. I went to North Beach and sat in Allen Ginsberg's favorite café and read one of his poems to assure me gay men mattered. The city was a living breathing organism and being out in it, I was part of it.

It wasn't just the Castro. It was all of San Francisco that allowed me to become a gay man and I owed my city for that. I spent some of the nights I used to spend in bars walking around neighborhoods I didn't know. I didn't expect it would make me a better person, but I had a sense of home than I never had growing up. On those nights, I promised to make sure that spirit of freedom in the city continued, so future generations of queer people would know what I knew. If I didn't make sure my community held on to that miracle that allowed me to be a gay man, it could disappear.

FIVE

Eddie asked me to drop by and when I did he opened the door with a smile. "Come on in and grab a seat. We need to talk."

"That sounds ominous."

Eddie sat across from me and rested his elbows on his knees. "I'll try to break it to you gently. I know you've been seeing a lot of Clay and I'm sure you love him, but what you're going through is what's known as limerence. It's that blinding first love."

"I just got up the nerve to tell him I love him."

"I know this hurts, but a few months from now you won't have the same passion. We all go through it."

"I love Clay." I started to tear.

"You do and I'm not saying you don't, but you have to trust me on this one, what you're feeling is fleeting and a couple months from now, you'll see it was just a mad infatuation. You won't stop loving Clay but you'll have a different kind of love for him."

"Did I piss him off?"

"Don't stress yourself. You did nothing wrong. Limerence is a curse from the gods. It has us loving someone and we think it's going to go on forever, and then the love stops."

"When we're making love, I know he loves me; I can feel it. It is the strongest feeling I've ever had for anyone."

"That's what first love feels like."

"Who are you to say I'm going to stop loving Clay? You haven't seen us making love. You haven't seen how tender he is with me."

"Kid, I know what you're going through."

"Wait a minute; did Clay say something to you? Did he tell you he's over our relationship and he didn't have the balls to tell me in person? Boy, that pisses me off."

"Hold on. Clay never said a word to me, and I'm sure he loves you."

"Then why are you making up this limerence thing?"

"Because limerence is real. You won't stop loving Clay, you'll love him differently."

"Love is love. Either I love him or I don't."

"I won't keep bugging you. Think about it and a few months from now when your feelings for him change you'll understand what's happening."

"That's a sour note to end my visit." I got up.

"Would you like some good news? Would you like to meet Bill and Jim?"

I sat down. "I'd love to. I've never met a gay couple and I'm going to ask them a lot of questions."

"Bill said they are going to the Grant Avenue Fair on Saturday. Can you wait that long? Stop panting like a dog."

"I'm not panting like a dog. Why do you tease me?"

We found Bill and Jim outside the Savoy Tivoli and Eddie introduced me. At first I thought they were straight men and I looked twice. I thought I was prepared, but I wasn't. With his coal-black hair and rugged features Jim looked like a model. Bill was equally good looking, taller blond and better built, and either of them would have shamed a room full of Hollywood stars. If anyone wanted a postcard with a gay couple to send to their suspicious relatives back home Bill and Jim would dispel their fears about homos being freaks. I looked again to make sure they were real.

After brief introductions on the street, where I shook like a leaf, the Tivoli's darkness was a welcome relief. Eddie passed around menus and I sat on a stool next to Bill at a tipsy metal table and leaned to him.

"How long have you and Jim been together?"

"We actually grew up just miles apart but we didn't meet until we both took the same class at Northwestern nine years ago."

"How long have you lived in San Francisco?"

"We re-connected when Jim came back from Vietnam."

"Were you already working here?"

"Yes, I was already working at the city planning department."

"And if one thing had changed we wouldn't have met," Jim said.

"What was that?" I asked.

"I was always to going to be an architect," Bill said.

"But he failed the engineering part of the exam."

"I failed it big-time, and I'm so glad I did."

Jim smiled at Bill. "Because he turned into this wonderful lover man."

"Do you have a secret for staying together?" I asked.

"I trusted him from day one." Bill said.

"We like playing house together and we like the same things," Jim added.

"But what about emotional ties?" I asked.

"I don't want to sound philosophical but no one knows the ways of the heart."

"So, you love each other."

Bill cocked his head and looked at me. "You act like that's strange."

"I thought I knew about love, but Eddie just told me my relationship with Clay wasn't going to last."

Bill looked me in the eye. "I barely know you, but please do not give up on love. It's the most astonishing thing we experience."

Bill asked, "It's noisy here, why don't we set a time for us to get together?

"I'm free later tonight."

"We'd like that, and I know Clay has a date tonight." Bill said. "Can you come around six?"

After our talk about limerence I should have seen this coming but I felt a twinge of jealousy. "I'd love to."

Bill and Jim lived in a beautiful Queen Anne Victorian on a steep block and I turned my tires when I parked. I walked under an arch dripping with wisteria and when Bill opened the door he'd changed to sweat pants and a T-shirt. "Welcome." He hugged me. "We just bought it and it needs a lot of work. Can I get you something to drink?"

"Juice if you have it."

"Back in a sec." He pointed to the adjacent parlor. "Jim's crazy for authentic Victorian furniture. He'll be down in a minute."

Jim bounded down the stairs and embraced me. "You made it! Let's sit." He snuggled next to me on rigid black oak sofa.

"Your home is beautiful."

"It has great bones."

"Eddie said you've been playing around with pleasure whatever that is."

"Following conventions never made sense to either of us and San Francisco was a place we could do a little experimenting," Jim said.

Bill handed me a tumble of juice. "We're interested in touching because touch is a primary way a man pleasures another man. Most well-balanced people were touched a lot when they were infants and our first response to danger is to grab another person."

"Men shouldn't feel bad when they acknowledge another person by touching him. It can be just a simple touch. We believe gay men grow as they get in touch with their bodies, and I'm exploring the ways yoga enhances the sexual experience while Bill's exploring how different mental states affect one's approach to sex. As he likes to say, a happy man enjoys sex more than a sad man."

"It's more complicated than that. Our bodies are controlled by our emotions and too often gay men use drugs to control their emotions. I'm looking for ways men can improve their state of mind when having sex without drugs. Something as simple as they way you shake their hand or hug them at the beginning of a play date can put a man at ease."

"I know this sounds crass, but does your science get in the way of your sex?"

Bill laughed. "It sounds scientific but we do it to enhance our sex and the sex we have with others. It may have wider applications, but we don't push it on anyone, we use what we learn to keep our sex life alive. If a man likes it, we're glad he wants to use whatever he learned from us."

"We're finding more and more men, even here, who are afraid of sex. It's a shame most people haven't accepted that pleasure keeps them healthy. Touching builds bonds, and there is nothing more reaffirming that holding another man; it says you're both important," Bill said.

Bill continued. "Men are afraid to even talk about sex. Last week a man got all fidgety when I asked about his sexual history, but when I told him I didn't know how to talk about sex when I came out he opened up."

"When they feel they have a sympathetic ear, some men have a lot to say and they feel good about getting it out, and that's nice to see," Jim said.

"I don't want to spend an evening with a man who's worried about paying the rent because great sex is a gift exchanged between men. There are so many differences among men there's no right way to start a date. Every man is different and that's part of the fun of playing with them, getting to know those differences. When we play, I do my best to adjust to their style so we all have a good time."

"We've gone through a medicine chest of drugs

seeking those that enhance our sexual experience. When I read about Ayahuasca I had to try it and Eddie knew someone in the Ecuadorian embassy and she snuck us into the country so we could try it."

"What's that?" I asked.

"Peruvian Indians use it. It's a dangerous drug so we did it with the man who wrote a book about his experiences with it. The drug is a hallucinogen that takes your mind on some wild, deeply personal trips," Bill said.

Jim said, "It was the most amazing trip of my life. I met my soul."

"What drew you to Ayahuasca?"

Bill showed me his palms. "We're only on this planet a few years, and if there's a drug that opens my mind and I can use it relatively safely I have to try it. I don't want to die regretting I missed something that profoundly changed the way I saw myself. But enough about us; what was it like for you growing up, Paul?"

"After Father died I stuck to myself and spent a lot of time in the library. Wisconsin is a piss poor place for a queer kid."

"It must have been rough for you and I'm sorry for you mother. What did you do for sex?" Jim asked.

"Let's say a jar of Vaseline got a good work out."

"Isn't it funny how nothing stops us?" Bill said.

"Growing up I thought gay men were weak and never involved in the big things in life, but here almost every man I've had sex with is trying to grow and they care about courtesy and humility but no one said a thing about having more courage than straight men."

"Coming out is natural for those of us who do it successfully, and we don't think about courage."

"What was your worst experience?" I asked as I moved closer to Jim.

Bill said, "It was a tall skinny guy on speed who had to try every position and I couldn't please him. Pleasure is a gentle thing and drugs keep you from appreciating its beauty."

"Is this something that came naturally?" I asked Jim.

"It's who we are. Those how-do books suck and poetry is a great way to know pleasure."

"A man's enthusiasm turns me on." I wanted to sound like I knew something about sex.

"And you're just beginning, Paul. Five years from now you'll look back and be surprised how much you've grown. Shall we adjourn to the bedroom?"

When I got to the bedroom I started loosening my belt and Bill told me to stop. Their undressing ritual caught me by surprise. Once he knew I was watching them, Bill began by opening Jim's shirt and pulling slowly it over his shoulder so I could see his nipples. He slowly unbuttoned the top of Jim's 501s and then opened each of the buttons below it. With his jeans at his feet, Bill began kissing Jim's back and as he reached his waist, he slipped a finger beneath the elastic of his white cotton underpants and with two fingers loosened them and helped them fall to his jeans. To take off Jim's boots, he pushed him onto the bed and spread his legs so I could see his crotch and Jim was hard. Bill raised a leg bent it and pulled his boot off his foot and put it on the floor. He used both hands to pull his sock off and tossed it to the side of the bed. After doing the same with the other boot Jim stepped so Bill could pull his jeans and underwear from around his ankles and toss them aside. They reversed positions and Jim began undressing Bill with the same dedication. When he finished undressing Bill, they stood opposite each other naked with their bodies glowing in the candle light. I started to undress and Jim stopped me. Bill asked with his eyes if he could undress me and I nodded yes, honored to be included in their ritual. I felt I was joining a gay fraternity. Naked I felt the brotherly closeness with them that I craved as a kid but never got. My erection was pulsing.

Bill told me to "Lie next to him." I lay next to Jim and Bill lay next to me. With moistened lips, I started kissing Bill with my arm around his shoulder. As we continued kissing, Jim took one of my legs, crocked it and put a pillow under my knee. "It's something I learned in yoga. It opens you nicely." I wondered if he did it because he thought I'd enjoy Bill's larger prick or if he enjoyed watching Bill play with other men. When Bill's sculpted body hovered over me I wanted him bad and I took his prick into my mouth and used all I'd learned to give him the pleasure he deserved. As I continued sucking ever deeper, Jim began circling my hole with his finger, and when he circled it from the inside, childlike joy radiated out from my crotch.

I was fairly new at getting fucked but it was an incredible wholeness that connected me to my deepest self. Playing with them was my chance to show Bill and Jim what I learned. I used one of those tricks after Jim fucked me with Bill's encouragement by resting Jim's ankles on my shoulders and bending him to where I was kneeling so his ass was opposite my crotch. I entered him slowly and once inside I twisted to change the angle of entry and that had him whooping.

We took a break, and the smoke from the joint we circled over us as we lounged on the floor. I was stoned to the tits and Gram Parson's *Grievous Angel* was crystal clear.

Bill picked me up by my shoulders, shifted me and rested me on a moving mat. Jim was next to me ready with poppers and lube. I took a deep breath and Bill began slowly slipping his fingers into me and each centimeter felt like a yard of happiness. He switched to slowly pulling his fingers all the way out and then pushing them back in. Each time his fingers went deeper. A final push got his hand go so far, my ass circled his knuckles and I gasped. He let me catch my breath and then he pulled his fingers all the way out, which was just as thrilling as him sliding them into me. "Holy shit!"

As I began to recover I felt his weight on my thighs and the pressure of his dick as it slowly parted my rosebud. Halfway into me Bill held his throbbing still until I had relaxed around it and once I'd relaxed he pushed all the way into me with his balls against my ass and I slipped into the unique ecstasy of being fucked. Bill sensed what I liked and when he got to my magic spot he applied extra pressure that released tension throughout my body and I started laughing. A few minutes later my climax was spectacular and I lay there until I stopped shaking.

"Nice!" Bill whispered.

My sex with Bill was serious man to man sex and with Jim I was dancing. We showered together. I stood at the door in jeans and a plaid flannel shirt and them in clean white briefs. I hugged them both. "I can't thank you enough for such a wonderful evening."

"You're a natural. We gotta do it again."

SIX

Eddie's invitation to his birthday picnic in Dolores Park included a handwritten note, *I want to talk to you.* It was usual enigmatic Eddie, but I suspected it had something to do with his ability to identify men with leadership qualities, something he'd been hinting at.

The air of Dolores Park held clouds of marijuana and the each of the hillsides had men in Speedos proudly showing off their bodies. I'd never seen so many happy men or this much flesh in one place and seeing them was insanely arousing. Someone on the other side of the park was playing Three Dog Night on his tape player and the whole park seemed to be keeping time to the music. I found Eddie wearing khaki gym shorts and a Polo shirt next to a galvanized bucket of iced Champagne. He along with some men I didn't know were drinking Champagne from plastic cups and passing joints.

I gave Eddie a big hug. "This is quite a bash. You said you wanted to talk to me."

He led me away from the group. "I would like to invite you a join a men's group. The group formed when I and few others were concerned about police brutality. One of the men was nice enough to let us meet at his home in Point Reyes Station and since then we've called ourselves the Station Men. Each man in the group started a community organization. One started the gay marching band another founded a gay health information center. We are making sure the community has the social infrastructure we need to survive as a community."

"Why are you asking me? I'm just a guy who makes friends with sex. Doesn't everyone?"

"I'll grant you make a lot of friends, more than most of us, but you also have started a collection."

"Can you tell me more about who's in the group?"

"Your collection is going to be critical going forward and we can help you grow it. Members of the group are here today to party which is already crazy. We have a three-day retreat in May, and that's when new men become members, so I suggest you put off meeting them until the retreat. It's a much better venue to get to know them."

"You're sure I'll fit in?"

"Cut the modesty. There's a table full of food and drink. Go enjoy yourself." He chucked me under the chin.

Clay walked up with a tin of home-made chocolate chip cookies. "The chocolate's melting so I need some place in the shade."

"Put them over there. Paul, would you be kind enough to ask that other group to join us?" Eddie asked.

"Do you have enough? And why all the smiles?" Is everyone on acid?"

Eddie waved his hand. "There's more than enough and they're smiling because for the first time they can love without shame. Where's your smile?"

A man with a trim beard and red shorts walked up and kissed Eddie, "Can I fetch another bottle of bubbly?"

"Thanks. We'll need more than one. David I want you to meet Paul." Eddie smiled. David had brown puppy eyes, thick lips, and a swimmer's body. Eddie knew I'd find David irresistible, and I did.

"Hi David, I'm going to ask that other group to join us. You wanna come with me?

"Sure." We headed across the park and he said, "Clay said he's been giving you the grand tour."

"He's been super nice. We camped on the Navarro River and tripped on mushrooms."

"Aren't they the best? I did them with him over Christmas."

"On the Navarro River?"

"It's way too cold there. We tripped in the Conservatory of Flowers in Golden Gate Park and I couldn't believe the flower petals flitting around like Tinkerbell. Clay said you're doing something with books." He pulled my ear playfully.

"I've started a collection of gay and lesbian literature."

"My cousin Lenny just turned eighteen. He doesn't think he's gay but I'm pretty sure he is and I've been trying to find him a good book, but I don't think there are many books for kids like him."

"How mature is he? *The Gay Mystique* chronicles the early, post-Stonewall era and was published last year. Do you think the title will scare him?"

"He's mature for his age and I'm willing to chance it with your book. We'll see if I'm right."

"If you give me your address I'll send you a copy. Let me know how it affects him so I can decide which books to collect."

He pulled a pen from his pack and wrote his name, address and phone number on the back of a match book and handed it to me. "Feel free to call any time."

"I might just do that." I didn't try to hide the tent in my pants.

"I was hoping you'd say that."

We got to the other side, and I approached a bear of a man. "You guys want to join our birthday party. Free food and booze."

He pressed me against his furry chest. "That's an offer a poor man can't refuse." He said with a hearty belly laugh.

On our way back, David took my hand.

Clay stood on a slight rise, raised a bottle of Champagne and tapped the bottle with a fork. He said in a loud voice. "Cheers to Eddie on his big fifty. He's welcomed most of us to Baghdad by the Bay with his special Eddie treats!"

"Here! Here!" I raised my cup and hooted and hollered with the others.

Eddie took a sip from his cup and tossed it over his shoulder. "Thank you all for coming. You are an incredible generation. More and more of you come every day to announce I am gay and I'm not ashamed! And you must have stopped along the way because you've been dusted with faerie dust that lets you fall in and out of love with ease, and I love watching you as your housemother."

"More like faerie godfather," someone yelled from the crowd.

Everyone laughed.

"As for my birthday, watching you build on our baby steps is the nicest possible present. I know you want to get stoned and make dates but take a moment and congratulate yourselves for doing something remarkable."

We raised our cups and cheered.

Eddie turned to Jim, "In your quiet way you and Bill are making history. What starts in your bedroom ripples out in ever wider circles and men like you are doing more to change the way gay men think about sex than a year of TV commercials."

"Why Mistah Butler, I have no idea what you ah talkin' about." Jim fanned his face with his hand.

Eddie went back to normal volume. "I want to thank all of you who are starting organizations that make our community one which has never been seen before, a community that you've designed explicitly for us. I don't know of any city or country where gay men and lesbians are not just welcomed but honored as we are in San Francisco. In a few short years, you've made the Castro a neighborhood as good as any in the city. Before you go home and do that thing you love to do when you get home and sometimes on the way home, take a few minutes and remember that each of you is making San Francisco a beacon of hope to everyone struggling with their sexuality."

We cheered again and I saw tears.

The crowd began to disperse and I stopped Eddie. "You have an incredible family."

"Come here."

We walked a few steps. "I want to thank you for

giving me the courage to drop my old friends. They were co-dependents and my social life was dinners at the home of the go-to decorator couple the Pacific Height's set used to decorate their homes. I went to all of them and they must have been the model for *Boys in the Band.* There were a lot of drunks at those parties and I could write the book on hang-over cures. I'm so proud of your generation that wants to make the community the best in the world and you don't give a hoot if someone objects."

"I'm glad you came out of it relatively unscathed. Will you ever talk to them again?"

"What would I say Hi, my name is Eddie and I'm an alcoholic? They wouldn't care."

"You're my hero."

"Look at you. You've become a star almost overnight. How did you do it so fast?"

"It was easy in a sexual democracy."

"Sexual democracy? Funny word."

"Naked men are equal and when a man's having sex with me he wants the sex just as much as I do and neither or us cares about any of the standard crap."

"If I may, what gets you off?"

"I'll be honest; a man who loves sex gets me off faster than anyone. After a couple questions about where he came from and what kind of sex he likes, I know if a man loves sex or if he just *has* sex. The difference is night and day, believe me."

"You haven't wasted a minute."

"If you'd lived in a very cold isolated place when your testosterone was just getting started you'd be fucking your brains our as fast as you could, too. The men who are the most fun are the men who are upfront about sex. When Jeff Botaky was in town we sensed that in each other our sex that night was some of the best I'd ever had and he's still the hottest sex."

"You didn't learn that at home. Can we sit? My legs are tired."

He brushed grit off a park bench and sat, and I got on my haunches in front of him and explained, "I have no hang-ups about sex and I'm not working out father issues so when I play all that matters is pleasing my partner. If he's not having a good time, I'm not having a good time. I think being clean emotionally scares some men but it keeps me sane."

"But you talk about sex openly. That takes all the mystery out of sex."

"The real mystery is why gay men are uptight about sex. I can't believe I'm the only man who wants good sex. Why do people step back when I say I want good sex? Gay men are not married people who have to put up with a husband or a wife who's lousy sex until death do they part. We can create our own relationships and yet I see men who still believe in the old crap. I say, shit or get off the pot! I suppose I should be generous with my brothers but why would anyone put limits on their ability to connect with another man? When I first said I wanted to *learn* how to have great sex, you acted like I was crazy. I'm no genius, but I've been here more than a year and I know sex is an art and art takes time and practice. Sex is also a language and a powerful connection, and one needs to learn how to harness them. Stuff like that doesn't drop out of heaven into a gay man's head. I recognize that playing it by ear from around twelve I may have grown up with fewer restrictions but if men are given a city and a community that allows them to drop all the crap around sex, they damn well better drop all the crap."

"You think men will change?"

"It doesn't happen overnight, but if men don't work on it, they get stuck in all the self-hating pettiness and back-biting I knew in Wisconsin. Great sex should be a joyous life-giving experience. That's what I came here for and that's what I work on every time I got home with someone."

"That's your lifetime goal?" He asked in disbelief.

"Come on, Eddie, you know me. I love one-upping the men I play with; if he can do that to me, I'll show him what I can do to him. My reward is seeing him just as pleased with what we've done as I am."

"How do you know?"

"It's all over his body. Haven't you been listening?"

"My life would have been so much easier if I'd

known what you discovered twenty years ago. It's been a long day. Thanks for coming. You made my birthday special and I'm outta here." He got up and took a last look at me before walking to his car.

I went home proud of standing up for my right to have great sex.

SEVEN

Bill wanted to talk to me about men who might fit in at a party he and Jim were throwing at a new second home in the Gold Rush country. He said on the phone, "They have to be men who are good at sharing. Can you stop by?" Knowing them, it could be the kind of party I dreamed of on long, cold winter nights with a sticky hand.

Jim was jumping around like a little kid when I got there. "You're gonna love the house. There's even a pond. We've been dreaming of a gathering for years."

"When we saw the house, we knew it was the perfect for a gathering. It can sleep ten with a huge kitchen that'll keep us fed and there are three showers and another outside. And best of all it's in the middle of fantastic forest."

"Sounds like quite the place." I asked, "Is it going to be an orgy?"

"That and more. We've played with remarkable men like you who love sex and want to give back to the community. What could be better than bringing them all together for a weekend so you can get to know each other?"

Jim added, "We don't have to abide by the old rules and since sex is an essential part of being gay why not combine sex with time to think about where the community is going?"

"You guys amaze me. Are there rules and what should I wear?" I hadn't realized it until they described the gathering, but it was just the kind of connection with the community that I'd been looking for.

"We expect cleanliness when men are playing and we're inviting men who are comfortable arguing over things like goals," Jim said.

"Paul, you've come along so fast you're going to fit right in. Jim and I wondered if you knew someone who'd be the right for that crowd. We've already invited Clay."

"I hope that's alright. Are you guys on good terms?" Jim asked.

"Clay and I had a long talk and I'm beginning to understand this limerence thing after he patiently walked me through it. It's still shitty! He still loves me."

"We originally had you rooming with Clay but we could switch you with someone else."

"I'll room with Clay. I don't want to lose him as a friend, and this will be a test."

"Where does that courage come from?" Bill asked.

"I know pouting's a waste of time but that didn't stop me from pouting for a week, but I can't imagine not having him as a friend."

"I'm glad you sorted it out because it hurts us when our friends are upset." He took my hand.

As we sat around a glass-topped table in their cheery kitchen with a great view of Dolores Park, Bill reminded Jim to tell all the guests to use the towels on the beds and strip the beds when they leave. When they talked about meals it sounded like they were planning elegant spreads that sounded too gay to me, I suggested every guest take responsibility for a meal. "It'll also give you more time to attend the weekend." I didn't know several of the men they'd already invited and said I'd share a meal with someone named Rusty. When they asked me if I knew someone who'd fit in, I suggested Richard Rhodes. We had sex regularly and because we knew we'd be lousy lovers I could do things with him I wouldn't do with Clay. It was clear from the way they talked about the party Bill and Jim saw it as a break-through, perhaps as something that epitomized the era. They encouraged everyone to not overdo it with clothing, to bring something spiritual they could share with the group and to come with an open mind. The more I thought about it the more I was convinced that the best thing that could come out of it was me being a brother with all of them. Bill hoped we might come together around a project, but I couldn't see men at a weekend outdoors being interested in sitting down and working out a fundraising plan for a new non-profit. When I left, Bill said I could ride up with him.

We crossed the Bay Bridge and past the Port of Oakland's cranes and idling ships. The road out of town was full of commuters on their way to work along with AC busses and trucks hauling goods from the port to distribution centers in the Valley and further on to Sacramento. The air was full of diesel exhaust. After crossing over Altamont Pass we drove through miles of orchards and I imagined playing hide and seek in the symmetrical rows of almond trees. When I asked Bill if he expected a fair amount of sex, he grinned. "You tell me, tell ten gay men take off their clothes and smoke dope and you know what they're going to do. What's best about his group is every man is someone we've played with so we know they will be comfortable in a group and you are no exception."

"I'm looking forward to meeting them."

"You'll have plenty of opportunities to do that. Once men drop their city persona I expect they'll want to share what's going on for them. It's going to be a special time, and we keep doing things as a community that no one else has ever done, but that won't last if we have no underpinning."

"Isn't that what Eddie's doing with the Station men?"

"It's going to take the whole community, not just the leaders."

"What's your fantasy for the weekend?"

"Jim wants to get a softball league out of it. I want the men to know that they can trust each other."

"They're both pretty big goals."

"I gave up long ago predicating what a group of gay men will do."

"Thank you for inviting me. It's going to be special."

We turned at an open metal cattle gate and I saw at the end of the drive a brown-shingled building with a rust colored metal roof and a wood deck as long as the house. Rattan chairs were arranged under brightly colored umbrellas on the deck and Jim hailed us from under one of them. "Glad you made it! Come on in, Paul. I'll show you your room."

Bill jumped out of the Jeep and embraced Jim. "Hi, sweetie. No traffic and the sun is definitely on our side this weekend."

I slung my pack over my shoulder. "I was expecting a log cabin but you've outdone yourself with this place."

Bill hugged Jim again and then led me through the vaulted living room with a stone fireplace to a hall. "You're in what we call the Lincoln bedroom. He opened the door to a bed with an ornately carved eighteenth century dark walnut headboard and an equally ornamented dark walnut footboard. Clay's bag lay open on the floor and his jeans and a T-shirt were thrown on the bed. "Clay's already here and I'm going to check on Jim." He left.

Jim was naked when he came back with Bill, and as he and I danced around the room, he pulled my T-shirt over my head and loosened my belt. "Our neighbors are so far away they can't see anything we do here."

"Sound travels, so we have to tone it down," Bill reminded him.

The foothills reminded me of being with Clay at the Navarro River, but I felt strong enough to deal with our new relationship. When I got to the front of the house I saw Richard and hugged him. "I think you're going to like it," I said with a smile.

"I'm glad to be here. What a great layout."

"Hey, Richard," Jim said with a twinkle in his eye. "Paul only says good things about you so you must be very bad. Let me show you your room," He took Richard's hand and they went into the house.

Bill introduced me to the guests around him on the deck. "I'd like you to meet Rusty Dragon. He works with homeless youth." Rusty was a redhead with a

South Boston brogue. I hugged him and he pecked my cheek. Then Bill said, "This is Gus Brody who grew up in New York and just got a job at the VD clinic." The man standing next to Rusty had long hair and a beard and he looked like Jesus. We hugged and I felt an extra pressure from him as we hugged. I was next introduced to Jeff Tackle and said, "Good meeting you, Jeff." He said, "I love being out in the sun." He pulled his shirt over his head, loosened the waist of his gym shorts and kicked them and his flip-flops across the desk. "This sure beats what Mormons have to wear. I left the church before they could excommunicate me." I liked his energy and once he'd stowed his bag we sat under an umbrella. I had a can of juice and we smoked a hash-laced joint.

My head was swimming at lunch when I was introduced to Tim Low with limbs of ivory and a sweet smile. I got up and we hugged and he said, "If you ever have a sick pet I just opened a pet hospital." Carl Frutchey standing next to him was dark-haired with French nose and I could tell his mind never stopped working. Out of the blue he asked, "Do you know string theory? I was just reading an article on the way up." I wasn't interested in his theory, but I couldn't avoid the bulge in his jeans.

When I went back to the room, Clay was unpacking and gave me a quick hug. "You sure you're OK with this?"

"I don't want to lose you as a friend."

At dinner, I watched Clay across a table laden with platters of fried chicken and bowls of vegetables. Each time our eyes connected, he smiled like he knew what I was going through. It reassured me but I wasn't sure what would happen in bed.

Bill stood. "Thank you all for helping us christen our home. We did our best to match you with, but if you want to switch roommates, talk to me after we finish here. Our primary rule is cleanliness when you play, but just as important is getting to know each other. We don't expect you to plan a revolution but you never know what happens when a group like this gets together. There's a hospital that's a twenty-minute drive if anyone has a serious injury. Does anyone have any questions?" I thought about asking Bill to reassign me but said nothing.

I didn't know how I was going to get through the weekend with Clay being there. I was going to have to be careful about how much I played. I was interested in getting together with Jeff and Gus had given me an extra hug. Then it dawned on me, how am I going to react when I see Clay slip away with a guest? Isn't that the test all horny gay men face? How do we accept our promiscuity in others? I attended the Unitarian church as a kid and felt unburdened by the rules other churches demanded of their believers, but dealing with Clay and another man wasn't going to be easy. Part of me felt

Clay was mine and I had some power over him.

I watched Clay as he got up. I expected he would come around the table and sit next to me, but he moved a couple chairs up his side of the table and sat next to Jeff and I overheard him talk to Jeff about the outdoor shower. Were they going to shower together? I recoiled at the idea of Clay and Jeff entwined under rivers of water.

"You OK?" It was Jim.

"Been thinking about ..."

"You don't have to stay with Clay. Why don't you change rooms? I can do it in a minute."

"Can I be honest?"

"Sure, let's step outside."

In a shady corner of the deck I said, "If I move, Clay's going to think I don't like him."

"I'm sure he will understand."

"I don't want to be seen as some in-your-face queen."

He put his arm around my shoulder. "We're all friends here and I can't think of a better group. Being honest with your emotions is the manliest thing a man can do. Do you want to me to talk to Clay?"

"No, it's something I have to do."

Clay was coming out of the bathroom, and I stopped him in the hall. "Can we talk?"

"Are you bothered about the room thing?"

"I'd like to change. But we'll still be friends."

"I see you're coming around on the limerence idea."

"Thank you. I'll collect my things." I was relieved he talked about the room and I didn't have to confess my jealousy. Jim put me in a room with Rusty.

Back at the table Gus talked about not coming out to his parents, and that started an argument between those of us who believed gay men are different from straight men in fundamental ways and those who thought we're just the same except for what we do in bed. Gus was a fervent advocate for us being fundamentally different. Tim Low talked about the pressure family and culture put on all Chinese gay men, and was more sympathetic to his seeing us as just like other men.

That was something I debated on those long, cold winter nights. With nothing more than Greek mythology to work with, I *felt* I was different from straight men. Part of that came from never being as confident as a straight man. Being gay had to be more than conditioning. Try as I might I was never as confident as my straight school mates. It didn't help that Mother kept mourning Father's death and kids at school called me egghead and nerd. On a long, cold February night I didn't think I could make it through another long, dark sub-zero winter. One of the women at the church saw me crying in a back pew the next day. She didn't ask me what was going on but she knew I was upset and gave me a quote by Rabindranath Tagore that

I thumbtacked on the cork board above my desk.

I have become my own version of an optimist. If I can't make it through one door, I'll go through another door—or I'll make a door. Something terrific will come no matter how dark the present.

His words got me through that winter and I returned to them that night. I was embarking on the most amazing journey of my life and I was interested in sex and talking about sex because they were essential to me. They weren't to other people, and I had to find strength somewhere inside me to deal with that. Being a gay man in San Francisco wasn't going to be easy.

Rusty and I sat in the shade of a towering pine and I sensed his genuine interest in helping the homeless man he befriended as a kid. Neither of us said anything but we fell into each other in the gentlest way. When we kissed, I felt his compassion for the homeless man. We tumbled around and took care of each other for an hour. I came back to the house and Jeff kept looking at me. I liked his energy, but I didn't know what he did with it. Once my libido took over I said, "Did your parents object to you leaving the church?" He led me to a shady grotto where he talked at length about his family and his relief when he left the church. He was no stranger to touch and once we took our clothes off he showed me a new way of being free with my body and he loved when I teased him.

When we sat for dinner Gus read a poem about an

imaginary friend who falls in love.

"That's very sweet. Can I guess who the boy is?" Bill asked.

Carl said, "If we are ever going to get our rights we can't just stay in the Castro and think the world will come to us; we have to elect gay men and lesbians to the Board of Supervisors." Jim wasn't as enthusiastic. "I think that would just piss them off." Gus argued, "We're just as good as they are, so why aren't we doing something about it?"

"I've started a collection of our literature and Thomas Paine's *Common Sense* started the Revolutionary War."

"That's a great idea," Bill said. "If we want to make a difference in that big bad world I can't think of a better way to start."

"I wish I there'd been a book about a boy like me when I was coming out," Gus said.

After dinner, we gathered around the fire pit and men started pairing off and wandering into the darkness. When Clay left with Carl, I grabbed Richard's hand and we lay on the air mattress on the deck. I always had fun with Richard, and that night he was into bottoming and his enthusiasm got me going. We took a break and I sat on the deck with juice and a joint and watched Gus and Tim wander off. When I got up to pee I passed Bill and Jim and Gus who'd just been playing in the master bedroom. Later I heard Jim's deep moans in the night. I didn't know who he was playing with but from the sounds they were making and crack of a whip I knew they both were having a good time.

Rusty was already in bed when I came in and I was still wet from the shower and slid into bed as quietly as possible. Hearing his breath and smelling his musk it was impossible for my cock to stay soft and I had a hard time keeping my fingers from sliding down my side and letting the back of my hand rest against him. Somewhere in the middle of the night I felt him move against my hand and then he rolled over. His lips were full and he let me chew on them. I flew my hand lightly over his body and in the moon light I could barely see the sea of freckles that covered his chest on down to his pubes and morning sun confirmed they were just red as his hair.

At breakfast Clay sat next to me. "You sleep OK?"

"I was exhausted."

"I saw you playing."

I wasn't sure how to say it. "Are you OK with that?"

"We're big boys. You're just getting started, Paul. You might want to find a way of not getting too attached to the men you play with. I know you want them to be your friends, but they have other friends, and there are limits; you can't be friends with that many people."

Growing up I had few friends because I didn't like the kids I grew up with. The only sport I liked was the gymnastics that I saw on television. The shapes of their muscles turned me on and I imagined touching them and their reactions to my touch that went from a sweet smile to a look of horror. My first friends as a kid were my movie heroes Alan Ladd and Cary Cooper. When I thought about the future I wanted friends that I could drop in on without calling, someone who would sit down and listen to my saddest tale. All he had to do was listen in a way that I knew he heard me.

When I got to Hanover I badly wanted a friend but the gay men there were fussy queens and when I said I'd never heard of Sondheim they treated me as an outcaste. Most students came from the East Coast and hung around together, and I understood why they stuck together; I would, too, if I had friends. Clay was the first man who seemed to understand me and didn't judge me. With him I could test the boundaries I grew up with and say what was on my mind and I could have opinions.

Would I be a good friend? I wasn't sure. I liked my privacy; I liked my apartment because I tailored it to the way I lived. For instance, I kept my bed next to the window to maintain my connection to living things outside of my room; this reminded me that I was alive and, more importantly, that I had come to San Francisco to do something.

As I rode home with Richard, I asked, "What did you think of the weekend?"

"The group was powerful but I felt sorry for Tim. It can't be easy for him as a gay man, but he's committed to that hospital."

"Bill and Jim did a great job of finding just the right men and just being there made all of us family." I said.

"I hope they do it again. I want to see Tim and Jeff."

"Clay and I patched it up."

"Why do you do that to yourself? I'd never be just friends with an ex."

"It was the hardest thing I've ever done."

"Why are all shitty decisions forced on us?"

"I think it's because gay men care about each other."

"But I think you may care too much."

EIGHT

Falling in love with Clay was the thrill of a lifetime but it didn't end well. I was new at relationships, and after mine with him, I wasn't sure if I'd ever be ready for another one like the one I had with Clay. When I thought about my future, I knew I wouldn't be as attractive in five years as I was then. San Francisco offered me an opportunity any gay man would give his left nut for, to have sex with men whenever I felt like it and the weekend at Bill and Jim's reminded me there are men who loved sex, just the kind I hoped I'd find. Why not take advantage of that? I wanted to have as many gay experiences as I could, and I was in the best possible place to do that. I decided I would get out there

and try every kind of sex that interested me. So far, I
hadn't got hooked on any drug and I had confidence I
wouldn't get hooked on one kind of sex. I wasn't sure
where my journey would take me but in March of 1972
I embarked on a sexual exploration.

In 1972 gay bars in San Francisco were the life blood
of the community, so they were my starting point. They
were the also community center and the church where
we worshipped. They were the center of style and the
first place that a new man in town went. Some, like Toad
Hall, had national reputations, and visitors had their
picture taken in front of the bar to show their friends
back home that they'd made it to gay Mecca. Most
important, gay bars were the center of social life; that's
where I made dates to play. After last call, the sidewalks
around gay bars got slippery with testosterone.

At first, I found the bars were overwhelming; the
mass of gay men pressed together with enough sexual
energy to blast through the walls intimated me and I
assumed the men knew what they were doing sexually.
If Scott hadn't taken me, I'm sure I would have stood
outside, afraid to go in, and even when we did go in,
I was amazed at the men's ease; they could have been
walking into a Woolworth's.

Bartenders were rock stars. They were the center of
attention and some made the most of it and acted like
the master of ceremonies. If I wanted to know where
to find the cheapest 501s or a treatment for the sore

on my dick, I asked a bartender. Bartenders were also confessors and they heard my tales of woe. They were also the repository of local gay history. If a bartender gave me free drinks, it meant I was special and that ranked me a notch higher on the acceptance scale. If I were the boyfriend of a bartender I would get instant membership with the *in* crowd, although San Francisco was so fluid that mattered little to most men.

My taste in men was blue collar because blue collar men didn't give a shit about therapy, labels, the schools I went to, or the current value of my real estate. I was sexually versatile and skilled as both a top and a bottom player, but if I had to pick one, it would be bottom because I loved having my ass played with. I was dependable because if a friend needed sex and called me, I was likely to say yes because my schedule at the travel agency was flexible and the owner was indulgent.

I designed my bedroom for sex and going home with men was a great way to get ideas for outfitting it. After plating the walls with shards of mirror, I moved my bed against a wall and found a large mirror in a second-hand store and hung it on the wall. The men I went home with were also incredibly creative in making the most of the little cash they had in designing their homes and seeing what they'd done with their home gave me ideas for decorating mine.

The first thing I did when entering a bar was to take

its temperature, a measure of the sexual energy. If, for example, there were two masculine men who were having a great time it raised the level and word would get out because that kind of energy was attractive. Some bars had established levels, like Febe's with its leather clad statue of Michelangelo's *David*. It had a regular clientele of slower moving older leather men. Most bars on Polk Street had high-spirited, generally younger men who were more interested in Cher than having sex. Some of the earliest gay bars were in the Tenderloin near the Greyhound Terminal, but the streets there were home to addicts, prostitutes, hustlers and serious alcoholics, so I never went there. Disco was just starting and I went to a couple discos and stopped. I went to the bars to meet men, and I didn't like sitting around until the music stopped and then going home with my date who was so worn out from dancing he had little energy for sex. Many men who went to discos used speed or a variant and I wouldn't go home with a man on speed because I wanted to enjoy great sex with men, not their drugs.

In the beginning, it took drinking three beers before I could talk to someone. As I drank them and smoked the occasional Camel I watched to see how the men met each other in bars. The men in back were usually there to have sex. It took time to perfect the art of starting a conversation and I was put off when a man asked if he could buy me a drink, because it smacked of privilege.

I wanted me and my partner to start on an equal footing and I usually simply introduced myself and asked if he wanted to come back to my place and smoke a joint. Once there, I started with kissing and when I was lucky, I ended up on the bottom.

My evenings started around 9:30 at Toad Hall. The men were good looking and wore denim and hooded sweatshirts, and I loved their long hair and beards. Their apartments usually had gardens so I sometimes had sex under the stars. Many of them had some college so I could start a date with an intelligent conversation. All of them were very happy to be as far from Tennessee or Modesto or wherever as possible that made snuggling with them warmer. We shared oral and sometimes anal sex. It was the most popular bar in town, so it attracted newcomers, and I loved meeting a man who was as excited to be here as I was when I first arrived. It gave our sex an added excitement. On Sunday, the line stretched around the corner of Star Pharmacy but despite all the men, it was the hardest day for me to make dates. On weeknights, the men were there for sex, so when we got back to my place we dispensed with small talk and played on my waterbed. I went home with a man whose home looked like a florist shop with plants on the floor and more in macramé baskets. His bedside table had incense, poppers, massage oil and patchouli oil. Once our serious sex started he reached for a small can of Crisco and the roll of paper towels kept on a shelf next to his waterbed.

If I didn't make a date at Toad Hall I went to the Rainbow Cattle Company. It had a somewhat older and rougher, brown-leather crowd. Amidst its great music, I might meet a man who'd moved to the country but came back for sex. They moved because either they wanted to grow dope or they moved with a lover. They were among the finest players and offered me a complete repertoire, ranging from long massages, deep-throat cock sucking, to fucking, and kink sex.

If I didn't make a date at the Cattle Company, I went to the Stud. That's where I met Clay, and he was often there talking about a new demonstration and he introduced me to potential dates. The bar became my favorite because it had the broadest types of men, everyone from men with pierced ears in bell bottom jeans to drag queens in opera stockings and platform heels with lots of eye makeup and glitter in their beards. It was a good place to find acid. Drag queens were hot sex and most of the other men I met at the Stud loved sex and they were experienced and patient teachers.

Over the course of two years I had sex with two hundred and seventeen men and three of them bring back the fondest memories. Tommy Doyle was five foot ten with short blond hair. His arms and legs were constantly in motion. He played classical piano on a black baby-grand Strauss piano that sat in the middle of his living room. He played Chopin, Shubert and Debussy with more feeling when he was stoned. He was the first man to fist me. He was very careful about how we went about it and always made sure I was comfortable. He started small with fingers and since I already loved dicks in my ass I was ready for a step up in sensation. As we began he moved his hand ever so slowly without pushing into me and without me doing anything except breathing. It took him three times of trying to get his hand in me. It took concentration, but instead of forcing muscles, I had to trust him and relax the muscles in my ass. I'd be lying if I said if it didn't hurt. The first time it hurt like hell, but oh how sweet it felt when he was inside. I felt I owned my whole body, and I was dancing on his hand. Tommy could be ready to fist in twenty minutes, a record.

Anders Erikssen introduced me to S&M. He was six foot four, blond, blue-eyed with perfect skin and just enough rose in his cheeks to make him an Arian god. He was so perfect, I was afraid to approach him. He saw me and smiled, and I realized men like him get a lot of attention but he wanted to be treated like a regular guy. We started with shots of vodka at a table with chairs that fit the contours of my spine. After we talked about what he was going to do, we sat on the flat bench sofa with rectangular bolsters in his living room with air thick with fir incense. I was seeing an acupuncturist, so I wasn't afraid of needles when he passed the thinnest needle through a flame to sterilize it. Then he made sure I was ready and he kept eye contact with me when he pinched one of my ball sacks and then he turned to watch as he slowly passed the needle through the pinch. I felt a sharp, quick pain. I didn't do poppers, and he kept slowly and carefully setting the needles until I had eight in my ball sacks and I felt a generalized warmth that radiated out from my crotch. Anders was a man of few words, but he did say, "Good for you" when I was dressed and at his door.

Andy Juric was short, dark and hairy and lived in Mendocino County. He had the body of a muscle builder and the dark hair on his chest looked like it had been designed to follow the contours of his torso. I saw him at the Kabuki Baths on a night I went there with Clay. We both noticed him the second he walked into the main hall. When all three of us were in the large, hot pool, Clay and I we introduced ourselves, and he said he wasn't sure he was gay. I didn't move on him and neither did Clay. When Clay was getting a massage, I followed Andy into the sauna and after several minutes of silence, I looked at him and he must have sensed it, because he turned to me with the face of a lost child. I asked him about his journey, and at what I thought was the right moment, I invited him to come home with me. There we talked for some time and I asked if I could give him a foot massage. As a Pisces I knew feet, and the massage put him at ease and he relaxed. When I massaged his thigh I carefully avoided his erection. I finished the massage, and when I lay back, he grinned and kissed me. We then took care of each other, and I was proud of connecting Andy with his sexuality, but Clay never forgave me.

For those two years, I was carefree and exhilarated as I shared with lovely men our common enthusiasm of being free to be ourselves. They shared the most vulnerable part of themselves with me, and they were my friends. We wanted our lives and the lives of those around us to be as loving as possible as we rode the wave crashing the shore of a spectacular city. My only wish was that my gay brothers everywhere could know the love we knew.

1973

NINE

I never forgot Michael. The sight of him behind the bar when I first got to town kept popping up, often when I was in the shower and it happened once when I was waiting for Muni. He was so full of life with his cockeyed smile and I knew my attraction to him came from somewhere deep; it was more than physical attraction, it was spiritual attraction; someone had determined we were destined to meet. I didn't believe in hocus pocus, but the feeling that Michael and I would be lovers every time I felt it was as real as my hand. Some force on high decided, perhaps before we were born, that I, Paul Bullen, would live the rest of my life with Michael Schön. A boyfriend had kept us from meeting, but the time had come. When I thought about it, I wasn't sure if I'd taken the couple years to get ready to meet him or not, but I had. I'd enjoyed almost every form of sex, so I was sure I wouldn't disappoint him there. I was less sure of being able to meet his emotional needs, but I trusted that when we met this time, he would be as sure as me that we were destined to live together. Full of hope I got out of bed, took a shower and called Bill and Jim and asked them to make good on their offer years ago to introduce us.

That afternoon I knocked on their door. Bill opened it with a smile, "Come on in. Michael's in the other room and can't wait to meet you."

"Thanks for setting this up."

"When I told him I was inviting you to dinner he had that smile of his; he knew exactly who you were."

"Michael, I'd like to introduce Paul." Jim said.

I stuck out my hand, and he grabbed it and pulled me into a hug. "I never forgot your hazel eyes. We're finally meeting."

"I'm so glad we're finally doing this." Holding him I was in heaven.

Dinner in their dining room epitomized what made San Francisco San Franciso for me, the perfect setting for our meeting. We were four gay men dressed in flannel shirts and jeans that they belonged to factory workers and we were eating a gold crusted roast and emerald spears of asparagus and golden Hollandaise sauce in a home once owned by *Ustis W. Blandchard III a man of high moral character* according to the brass plaque at the front door. I was seated next to Michael, and somewhere in the middle of the meal our knees touched. I don't remember who started it, but it became a game of us looking at each other out of the corner of our eyes and smiling. At one point, Jim caught us and nudged Bill.

After dinner, we sat in the front parlor with espresso in tiny cups. I asked Michael about his childhood and learned his mother died of cancer when he was twelve, and I could tell by his tone, that she was still a very important part of him. I made a few jokes, and Michael roared with laughter. I walked with him to the Muni stop, and along the way he told me when he was in high school, his boyfriend was sleeping with him in his bedroom until his step-mother found out. When I asked what happened, he said his father told his boyfriend to leave but Michael and his boyfriend bought a beat-up Chevy and drove to San Francisco with little more to their names than loose change. The car was coming and Michael asked if I'd be interested in seeing a cabin he was building. I said and I would, and promptly at nine thirty on a sunny Saturday Michael pulled up in his moss green Ford 150 and I got in. "Nice truck."

"It's my first, I bought it last week." It suited him perfectly. Michael personified masculinity. He was clumsy at times but that made his masculinity all the more natural; it seemed to seep from every pore in his body. I'd never seen a gay man like him. I'd longed for that kind of sureness as a kid and he was completely unaware of it.

Michael's plywood shell of a cabin sat alongside a creek at the bottom of a canyon of dark green pine sentries. The air held the heat of the day and the sky was the blue of the ocean. Standing next to him I felt some of his pride in building the cabin with his own two hands. He said, "Let's go down to the creek and smoke a joint." Who was I to argue? This was my dream come true.

We stripped and I followed him down the sandy path. I stood in the creek surrounded by a jungle of undergrowth filled with tiny birds and buzzing insects. I took a hit off the joint and lay back on the tall grass. He said, "Friends from the bar have been helping with the cabin but I wanted this weekend to be just us."

"Is there something I can do?"

"I'm going to get us some drinks and then I want to lie next to you in the sun."

I spread a beach towel and when Michael came back he said, "I dreamed of you."

"That's nice. Did you really?" I hadn't expected he would think of me.

"I dreamed I met a special man in a faraway land."

"I have this feeling we knew each other in a prior life," I said.

"Kinda the same thing. Maybe we are supposed to be doing this." He began applying sun tan lotion to my forehead.

"What's your sign? I'm Pisces."

"So am I. That may explain it. We're intuitive."

He put his lips to mine, the sweetest kiss of my life. I slid closer and we began making out. Holding him I was holding my future. Whatever I did to him, like stick my tongue in his mouth, he did in return. From then on I wasn't paying attention to what we were doing but we moved seamlessly whenever we shifted positions, we were one body having a wondrous time in the sun. His cabin became a partner in our dance of lust.

After a dinner of perfectly broiled pork chops and salad with artichoke hearts and slices of a white cheese, we smoked a joint on the deck. I gazed at the stars. "I feel so small yet part of something huge. Did you ever think of something like this growing up?"

"I knew I was going to build my own home. I didn't know where."

"I'm glad you decided on here."

"And I'm glad you decided to come here."

That night I had the best night of my life. We were gentle with each other and we pushed each other at the same time. We made love all over his cabin, lying down, standing up, and splashing around in the creek under a full moon. I woke snuggled next to him tangled in a sleeping bag on the deck.

He made bacon and eggs for breakfast and without explanation, he wandered off. I spent the day getting a sun tan, worrying about where he'd gone. He came back as the sun was turning orange at the far end of the canyon carrying a fistful of wild flowers that he stuck in a clean mayonnaise jar. He said little during dinner. We sat on the edge of the deck and smoked a joint. He looked at the stars and said, "Thanks for waiting. I needed time to think. My friend JR is moving to the river with his lover and he asked me if I wanted his quite wonderful flat in a restored Victorian. It's too big for me, and I wondered if you'd be interested."

"I would."

"I've had steady reports from men at the bar about your comings and goings. You have a reputation."

"So, you know I go home with a lot of men."

"Why do you do it?"

"I like to make men happy. Touching a man also makes me feel I'm worth something. I know it sounds weird but unless I'm in tune with the man I'm playing with, it's not worth the effort."

"But you never stop."

"I learn something from every man. Growing up in a small town I wanted to get out of there as fast as I could because more exciting things happened in big cities. I felt I was missing something, and I had to live in a city where things were happening, and once I started dating, I wanted to meet as many men as I could."

"So you wouldn't miss something?"

"They also fill a hole, and I don't mean it that way. I felt hollow as a kid. I read every book in the library to fill it, but filling it with information wasn't what I needed. I know it's embarrassing but I need affection."

"Like this?" He pushed me back onto a towel and snuggled next to me.

"Just like that," I whispered into his ear.

"We can try living together. It will be a test."

"I'm willing if you're willing."

"You know I am."

What I remember of the rest of my time at his cabin was that I was floating on air. We anticipated each other's every desire, we got up to shower in his outdoor shower at exactly the same moment and I knew before he asked that he wanted me to wrap my legs around him. Time had no borders and our existence extended all directions. It reinforced my feeling that we'd known each other in another life. I didn't see us together in a foreign country or another time in history; it was a spiritual connection. After saying it once I never raised it again because I was afraid he would try to fix the time or place it happened and it wouldn't sound right to me. Whatever the feeling was, it was strong that our souls were together in an eternity or we started as the same soul. That night I dreamt I was leading a parade with Michael and he was holding a picture of me and Michael leading that parade.

Michael was giddy when he took me to JR's flat. The blue and cream exterior made the building stand out on the street. The work inside was done by craftsmen and the moldings and the wide-plank floors looked original. The flat had three bedrooms, a dining room and a living room at one end of the flat and an enclosed porch at the other end. A month later, after painting my office and the smallest bedroom, I stood in the shower of my new home, in a cloud of steam. I knew the test was just beginning.

TEN

This was my first birthday in San Francisco and it turned into one of the most amazing nights of my life. It started when Michael told me he was taking me out to dinner and said I should wear the cowboy boots and Stetson hat I bought at a street fair. That seemed very strange and it got stranger when we pulled up to the entrance of the Mark Hopkins hotel, one of the finest in the city. We were greeted by a silver-haired man in a tuxedo who welcomed us like he was an old friend of Michael's before he ushered us into the hotel and then through a plush lobby with a tropical wood reception counter to an elevator marked private. I couldn't understand why we were in the hotel much less why we, two queer men in cowboy gear, were riding in the hotel's private elevator. It got weirder yet when he got out of the elevator and I saw men in dark suits with earpieces outside the only door at one end of the long hallway. This had to be a set-up. Michael had been duped into coming to the hotel so the feds could arrest him for the pot he grew at his cabin. Being stuck in a cell was my greatest fear, but it didn't faze Michael to be dressed like a cowboy when he walked through the trappings of a fine hotel. He didn't care that people would be staring at two men that stuck out like a sore thumb; he acted like the Mark Hopkins was his second home. My fears were allayed when the man in the tuxedo took us to the opposite end of the hall and my fears disappeared when the door opened to an opulent penthouse suite.

Rich people's sense of entitlement unsettled me. They had a power over everyone they believed they were superior to even though I knew they were no better than me; they just had more money. Michael sat beside me on a plush sofa covered with chintz and asked me to get him an apple.

"Where am I going to find an apple?"

"Over there." With a twinkle in his eye he pointed to a cellophane wrapped basket of fruit on the side table. I used my pocket knife to tear open the cellophane that cried when it ripped it open. I plucked an apple from the tower of fruit and tossed it to Michael. When I went back for an apple for me I saw was a stack of telegrams next to the basket.

Michael said, "Open them. They're for you. Friends from the bar want to wish you a happy birthday."

I was touched when I opened a dozen humorous telegrams from people who knew me only as Michael's current boyfriend.

Michael turned in horror. "I bought dope but forgot papers."

"Not a big deal. Call room service."

"What will they think?" I'd never seen Michael frightened.

"I'm sure they've gotten weirder requests."

Michael called the concierge and ten minutes later an attractive eastern European man delivered a silver plate with two packs of paper. After presenting the tray he bowed and backed out. Michael took the packs to the sofa and proceeded to roll two joints and laid them on the glass topped coffee table like an offering to the gods. We smoked one and fell back on the sofa. I had just gotten as far as opening the brass button on the top of his 501s when there was another knock on the door. I froze but Michael calmly went to the door opened it a crack and whispered something to whoever was outside. He came back. "I told them to serve dinner at seven. Is that OK with you?"

"What's going on?"

"Peter Donovan, the man who met us at the door, is an old friend from the bar. When I told him I wanted to do something special for your birthday he offered this suite. He couldn't tell his boss we were two gay friends, so we made up a story that we were estranged ranching brothers from Chico who were reuniting for the first time in years."

"We went through all that for me?"

"You deserve it."

I was too taken aback to argue. "Can I look around?"

"It's your night." I took my time as I walked around the suite inspecting the two elaborately decorated bedrooms and the two adjoining bathrooms with their tiled shower stalls and huge pedestal sinks. Finally, I inspected a solarium that hung over the side of the building and with a spectacular view of the East Bay shoreline and the lights on their hills.

Promptly at seven another knock on the door, Michael told him to enter and a good looking young man in a *toque blanche* wheeled in a cart with two silver domes on top and fine china and silver on the lower shelf, moving it aside a table set for two.

I moved one of the chairs so I would be sitting next to Michael. Once we were seated the young man used silver forks to transfer slabs of filet mignon to our plates and then with silver spoons he filled our plates with green peas and bright yellow carrots. The young man showed Michael a bottle of red wine and poured some into a goblet. Michael took a sip and nodded and the young man filled his goblet and then mine. "Will that be all?" the young man asked. He was young and fresh and I wondered what he thought about two men sitting next to each other.

"Thank you. We're set." Michael said and the young man turned and left. Michael took my hand. "What would you like to do?"

"I can't wait to taste this delicious meal and then I want to make love to you in every room of this incredible suite."

"I brought acid we can do after dinner."

No one had ever done anything close to this for me. Mother treated birthdays as a necessary duty so my birthdays were loveless. I had to accept there was something about me that Michael liked enough to plan an elaborate party. Was I the man of his dreams? Had I duped him into thinking I was capable of love?

Surprise birthdays in fine hotels were the stuff of Hollywood and gay San Francisco kept surprising me; nothing was out of bounds as long as it created beauty or made someone happy. What's the foundation of that philosophy? Nothing that good can last. I kept thinking it was a dream and I would wake up, but instead I felt more alive and didn't want to waste a minute of being with Michael. I thought love was other people's emotion, not mine, but Michael turned that on its head. He thought I could be loved.

We dropped the acid and looked at windows of the hotel across the street. As I stood in my underwear I wondered if a man presumably straight in one those hotel rooms was having half the fun I was. Did he have someone in his life that showered them with love and celebrated his birthdays in a fine hotel? Standing next to Michael in underwear and bare feet I was the luckiest man in the world.

"Follow me." I took Michael's hand and led him to the master bedroom. My bare feet sunk into the plush carpet. In the room, I pushed him onto the down comforter and then joined him. We wrapped around each other and he pressed his thick lips to mine and then slowly worked his tongue around my gums. I was in another world as we rolled around on the bed. I pulled back and filled my hand with spit and Michael got up long enough to snatch a towel from the adjacent bathroom and put on the comforter and lay atop it. When the tip of my cock touched him, I held back, even when I want to plunge into him, long enough to make my entry slow enough for him to enjoy all of me. We made love in the second bedroom and I had just as much energy as I had when we made love in the first bedroom. Our sex felt natural as we moved from one position to the next and it happened so effortlessly what we did was a blur but it revealed our preferences; Michael was a cock man and I liked anal. What drew me to him was his ease with life and his calm when dealing with a bar full of attractive customers that each wanted a piece of him. He did that despite being raised by a single dad with little interest in his children and then being dumped by the man who came with him to San Francisco. Any man who went through kind of shit should be a little crazy but he wasn't. What I saw that night was the teddy bear who was scared of the dark and wanted to be loved.

Could I go on like this all night? When is enough enough? Or when love's involved, is it ever enough? We stopped to smoke a joint and I picked up a pillow and smashed it over his head. "Take that!" He squirmed away grabbed a pillow and knocked me back on the comforter. "Take you, you beautiful man!" To get some air I went to the outdoor patio and slumped on an iron chair. Michael pulled another chair beside me and lit a joint. When I exhaled, I saw a fire escape in the side of the building and I had to climb it. I pointed to the metal ladder. "I can't resist the challenge."

"Are you sure you want to do that?" Michael cautioned.

"You said this was my night." I started climbing without thinking that the cold metal was going to be painful on bare feet but reaching the top was my goal so I took the pain in stride. As I stepped on the second rung Michael yelled, "Be careful!"

"I know what I'm doing." As I kept climbing rung by rung by rung in my underwear like a carnival monkey oblivious to anyone in tall buildings. When I hung from the highest rung in my underwear, opposite to the diners in the hotel's finest restaurant who hated men like me, I literally had the upper hand.

"May I offer you a shower?" he asked.

My cock was pressed against his butt as steam filled the chamber. I used my finger to draw a heart on the shower door and whispered, "I love you."

Michael drew an arrow through it and whispered, "I love you, too."

I couldn't take my eyes off Michael he toweled off. He had the perfect physique and I imagined him back at the cabin making love to me. No gay man ever had it so good.

"My turn." Michael took my hand and led me back to the living room where he opened a box of See's chocolates. "Which would you prefer, kind sir, toffee or dark chocolate cream?"

"How good of you to ask. I think I'll have the toffee." I did my best to sound British.

He put the toffee on my tongue and closed my mouth and I mumbled, "And what will you have, kind sir?"

"I'd like that crunchy looking thing," he said.

"I can't thank you enough for the most wonderful birthday party a man can ever have."

"You're my man." We fell back on the comforter and I dreamed the sweetest dream of me and Michael on a boat that drifting across a calm ocean under a blazing sun.

I woke with Michael whispering, "Your breakfast is waiting for you."

"Huh?" My mind was scrambled.

"There's eggs and sausage waiting for you in the solarium."

"When are you going to stop being so nice?"

"No time soon."

Eggs and sausage were my favorite breakfast and I celebrated my birthday with Michael at my side a second time as I looked out over the city that had been so good to me. There was another knock on the door. I scrambled to get dressed and by the time I got to the door the voice on the other side of the door said, "Your chariot awaits!"

Our kiss lasted the length of the trip to the lobby. In the truck, I said, "You sure know how to show a man a good time."

"I can't think of a better man."

The next morning while Michael slept I went to my office, put my feet on my desk, and closed my eyes and savored the most amazing night of my life, everything from my puzzlement at wearing cowboy gear to our making love in every room. Our sex felt natural as we moved from one position to the next and it happened so effortlessly it was a blur, but it revealed our preferences; Michael was a cock man and I liked anal. I also discovered a different Michael. What drew me to him was his ease with life despite being raised by a single dad with little interest in his children and then being dumped by the man who came with him to

San Francisco. Any man who goes through kind of shit should be a little crazy but he wasn't. What I saw that night was a teddy bear who was scared of the dark and wanted to be loved.

ELEVEN

Until I met Michael I had never loved a man, though I thought I had. Michael said he wanted us to have rings. I loved the guy but rings turned me off. I said, "You and I have something that's so special a ring will say we're just like straights." Then I went too far and added, "May I remind you we are not straight?"

"Rings say we love each other."

"I've loved you since the day I first saw you behind the bar."

"If we could get married would you marry me?"

I knew nothing of relationships. Growing up I didn't expect I would marry a woman and become a husband; I only thought about getting out of town. I said, "That's a hypothetical question." I opened the fridge and took out a jar of juice.

"You're not answering my question."

I sat next to him. "I'm not going to answer a hypothetical question. I never dreamed I would ever be in a place like San Francisco that practically forces me to be honest and what we have is *the* most honest man to man relationship. We are out to the world and we have no secrets. Why change something that's already perfect?"

"If you're so honest you should be able to answer my question.

"You are the best thing in my life and I want to spend the rest of my life with you. I don't think you know it, but you are a very special human being, Michael." I put my other hand on top of his. "I have no idea why you like me but I love exactly what we have and I'll be damned if I'm going to change anything that disturbs the balance."

"You make me sound like an equation."

"You are more than all the equations in all the text books in the world." Suddenly I felt overwhelmed and fought back tears. I couldn't put what I felt into words.

He looked into my soul. "I chose you because I love you. Isn't that enough?"

"It's more than enough. You are more than I ever hoped for, Michael. Maybe I just don't understand love." I couldn't make logical sense of the strange feelings swirling around in my head. Why did he have to mention rings in the first place?

He got up and held me. "I cannot tell you what love is, I could have it all screwed up, but I know I love you." He kissed the back of my head.

"Can't we just keep it like this?" I'd never I felt so vulnerable.

"I'm sorry this upsets you. Maybe it's too soon for rings."

"It doesn't mean I don't care for you. I crazy care for you!" Thankfully we had to meet Eddie, which brought the discussion of rings to a close."

Eddie's apartment was in an elegant apartment block in Pacific Heights that his mother owned. He waved us in with, "Come in. Come in."

"Thank you. Your home is very elegant," Michael said with a sense of awe.

His living room had an unobstructed view of the bay and once we climbed the circular staircase to the roof deck, the view was breathtaking. "Sit." Eddie pointed to a set of deck chairs. "I have a proposal."

I shifted my gaze to him. "I'm all ears."

"When you have enough books to fill a space, I will buy you a little storefront on one condition."

His offer stunned me. "That is very generous of you, and if I may be so bold, what would that condition be?"

"That you name it the Paul and Michael Collection.

Gay life is changing fast, and I want to honor what you're doing for the community."

I started to cry. This was a dream come true. No one had ever been so kind and generous. I hugged Eddie and then Michael joined the hug. "You have no idea how much this means to us, Eddie. I can't possibly express my gratitude."

"And I can't thank you enough for all you've done for Paul," Michael said.

"Being there on opening day will be more than enough. You do have to do one thing."

I looked up at him. "What would that be?"

"You have to accept a porno collection."

That came out of the blue! "How did you get a porno collection?" I asked in disbelief.

"It was Cyrus's, the boyfriend I told you about. He was the archivist at the Stanford Library."

"And he collected gay porno?"

He went to a bookcase and removed a few books. Behind them I saw another complete row of books.

"What an amazing way to hide a collection!"

"There's more."

Eddie led us downstairs where he opened a box and withdrew a faded poster deriding the evil homosexuality. "That's just one of several from the 19th century, when groups like the National Puritan Party infiltrated churches with their anti-gay hate rhetoric." He withdrew a faded editorial from the

Chicago Tribune from 1926 that protested a powder dispenser in a men's room at a public bathroom. "This kind of thinking was common throughout much of the early part of the Twentieth Century and Cyrus wanted to document it."

"Where's the porno?"

"The flesh is all over the collection. He opened another box of magazines with naked men on the cover that must have been twenty years old.

"What do you want me to do with all of this?"

"This collection needs a decent home. I'm counting on you to keep Cyrus's memory alive. He spent years amassing this collection and it must be preserved. He's part of our history."

"And you want me to include it in my collection."

"I can't think of a better place."

"I'm not worried about the nay-sayers. Once word gets out that there's porno in the collection men will be lining up. I am worried about having space. From the looks of it, it could take up half a room. There's also the problem of the books ending up soiled in the bathrooms."

"Your perverted mind thinks of everything."

"I was joking. The collection would be a real asset, and again, don't take that the wrong way. It would probably be the first porno collection ever."

"I know taking care of it will require archiving."

"What's that?"

"That's taking care of the collection. Your men's room comment reminded me that magazines like these are perishable."

"Holy shit!! More expenses."

TWELVE

As my collection grew in size and scope, it required more and more of my time. Between work at the travel agency, sex with friends and the collection, my time was scarcer than ever, leaving practically no time for Michael. Meanwhile, Michael had left his job as bartender and started the landscaping business he'd dreamed of. His landscaping became an obsession and it started to replace what little time he used to spend at home with me. Much as I wanted to support him, I worried our relationship could be in trouble if the situation didn't change. Michael was coming home with muddy boots, and I made allowances and quickly mopped the floor and didn't say anything. I wanted to be supportive, but then one night he came home long past dinner and I'd had enough. "This is the third time you've been late," I said.

"This client keeps asking for more," he said as if I should have expected it.

I sorted books and by the time I was done and came to the bedroom, he was sound asleep. When I snuggled next to him he just grunted and turned away from me.

The next day I proposed we go to a movie in the hope of rekindling our old desire. When he walked into the theater after the movie had started, my anger welled up. "What's your excuse this time?" I demanded. "You agreed on a movie."

"I'm here, aren't?" We didn't speak the rest of the night.

The next night he didn't get home until eight and I said as calmly as I could, "I know how important landscaping is for you, but your lateness is getting to me. I'm worried what it's doing to our relationship."

"Why do you keep nagging me? Do you think I want to work late all the time?"

"Michael, we haven't had sex since you started your business a month ago. Dinner was the only time I saw you and now we don't even have that. I admit I spend time at the storefront, but I make sure I'm home on time. You're the one who wanted rings. Have you changed your mind?"

He looked at me impatiently, "I can't fuck this job

up. I'm just getting started and it's going to lead to more work."

Much as I wanted to see his new career succeed, I was furious that he hadn't heard a word I said. "You still want to live with me? Maybe we should sell the flat."

"Look who's talking? Maybe I'd come home for dinner if you didn't need to go to the bars."

"Our sex is more important than my sex with friends, and I want to have sex with you just as much as I did when we met."

He flashed a disdainful smile. "You've gone home with men who aren't your friends."

"That only happens when I've had a bad day and then its first come first served."

"You continue to confound me," Michael said with resignation. "I think our sex is still the best, and I apologize, but gardening is what I've always wanted to do. You don't know how much I appreciate your help; I wouldn't be gardening if weren't for you. I owe you so much."

I saw my opening. "You want to play?"

"I'm tired, let's not drag this out." He kissed my forehead and headed for the shower.

Sex had been our strongest bond. It was the way were told each other the truth. I was lost when I tried to piece together what had just happened. I'd always heard relationships took work, but I didn't expect them to hurt this much. Our love had been so true, and I wrote off our argument about rings as just a tiff, but now it might have been the beginning of the end of our relationship. I don't know what got into me, but Michael sometimes went to Buena Vista Park, a popular cruising park, so I drove there in cool fall air and stopped in a parking lot of empty cars. I parked, looked around and wasn't sure why I'd come. Had I come for revenge? Once revenge had me it fucked me up but there I was in the park and I couldn't think of another reason other than revenge. I hated to admit that revenge was part of being in a relationship. Shit! I got out of my car and as I closed the door I saw a man walking his dog. "Hey good to see you," David called, "I haven't seen you since Eddie's party. I didn't know you came here."

"I came to get away. Michael and I are going through a rough time. Can we talk?"

"You want to come back to my place? It's just over there." He gestured to a building across the street.

As he made coffee, I checked out his bookcase that included large photography books and the classics, including Gore Vidal and Gide, so he had a good mind. He joined me in the living room with two mugs of coffee and gestured toward a chair. "I don't mean to pry, but if you'd like to talk about what's going on with Michael I'll listen."

I didn't want to talk about my problem with Michael with Eddie. "He's never home any more. You know, at first I thought he was seeing someone."

"You wouldn't be the first person dealing with a lover who goes out a lot."

"I wish it was that, but once he got started landscaping, he acts like I don't exist."

"That's a shame. He's a lovely man."

"He keeps promising me he'll be home on time but it pisses me off when he always gets there late." I was glad to get that anger off my chest.

"Are you sure he's not seeing someone? That's what it sounds like to me."

"I'm sure it's the gardening, and part of me wants to be happy because that's what he's always wanted, but I can't be happy when he shuts me out."

"You miss your special times with him, don't you?" It was as if he could read my mind.

"If you mean sex, you're exactly right. Our sex is always sweet and he knows my body and what I like better than anyone. That's why not coming home on time hurts so much."

"I'm sure that's difficult for you." He put a reassuring hand on my knee that took me to the time Michael did it that first night at his cabin. "I miss our sex so much."

David paused, as if gauging what he was about to say. "I know I'll never be as good as Michael, but I'd like to cuddle if that will make you feel better." David kissed my cheek.

David's lithe body had always appealed to me and I

trusted him. "That would be nice." I knew where this was going to end.

"Let's go to my bedroom? Would that be OK? I'll turn on the music."

Sitting next to him on the bed with Procul Harum in the background David pulled his shirt over his head. I did the same. We started kissing and I was getting the attention I was missing with Michael. It felt incredible. It wasn't just sex, it was intimacy. "You're a great kisser." He pulled me onto the bed with him.

He placed his hand on my erection and held it there. "May I?"

I raised my hips and he opened my fly. Once he had my cock in his hand, I reached for his dick and found he was just as hard as I was. We started stroking each other. He spit on my cock and we continued stroking. He was as talented as I expected, and I held back as long as I could but he kept stroking and kissing until I eventually I reached that point and I climaxed. I was always a responsible player and returned the favor by gently taking his thick, uncut prick in my hand. I began stroking it slowly and when I spied a bottle of lotion I stopped stroking long enough to cover my palm with lotion. I went back to stroking with a well-greased hand and he began to moan and I kept him on edge as long as he let me. Finally, I took him to the point where I could tell he was about to come and I would get my reward. I increased my stroking and he closed his eyes and threw his head back as his prick spewed jism as far as his nipple. He fell back gasping. "You sure know what you are doing."

"You know what they say, practice makes perfect."

There was a long pause. "Are you going to tell Michael?" I could see the concern on his face.

Unlike sex with friends, I felt something with David because he filled the emotional void left by Michael. I had to deal with that. "I have to think about it." I knew a situation like this would happen. Playing with friends was engrained in me and Michael, and I had an agreement that when I played with a friend, I had to be home by eleven. Now I had to decide how I was going to talk to Michael about my feelings for David and I was torn between being true to the finest man I'd ever known and satisfying basic human urges.

David put our empty cups in the sink. "I won't say a word, but I would like to see you again."

"I would like to see you again, too. You make me feel good about me." We hugged a long farewell hug.

When I got home my emotions were all over the map. Michael was sullen and the entire dinner passed in silence. I suspected he knew something was up, but I hadn't decided how I would tell him about David so I slept fitfully.

The next day Michael left to work while I was still asleep. Over a cup of coffee I debated should I call David or should I put an end to our little affair? After my second cup, my libido won and I phoned David. An hour later I was naked and enjoying David next to me, getting the affection I missed with Michael. No matter how I twisted the reasoning, I couldn't see a way of incorporating David into my life while I was still living with Michael. He had found his calling in gardening, and hoping he'd grow out of it was wishful thinking. Telling him I was playing with David was going to upset him and possibly end our relationship, but I had to tell him because I couldn't live with myself if I didn't.

That night when Michael sat down for dinner and I said, "I'm not going to beat around the bush. I've been seeing Eddie's friend David."

I saw the hurt in his face and I didn't know if he was about to cry or scream at me. "You think I'm worthless because I can't stop work and be with you?"

"I've never thought you were worthless but what am I supposed to do?" I resented him turning it around on me.

"Do you expect me to be ready for sex at a moment's notice?"

"I do when I've gone to all the trouble of getting ready. I can't live as half a partner where we see each other only when you make the time."

"This job is the most important thing I've ever done."

"Is it more important than me?"

He glared at me as he weighed his next words. "Mrs.

McKey said I can use her guest cottage whenever I need it and I'm taking her up on her offer."

"Don't say that." The thought of losing him froze me.

He stood. "You don't love me. You'd understand me if you did."

"I love you more than ever." I started to cry.

He headed toward the door. "I've had enough of your high and mighty attitude. Fuck you!" He stormed out, slamming the door.

That night I got so drunk, my head was killing me in the morning. I was a wreck and without bothering to call I went to see Eddie, who of all my friends would be most supportive.

"Eddie, I need to speak with you," I said at his door.

He stood in his bathrobe. "You show up unannounced, my eyes are barely open so this better be important."

I sat across from him on a mauve loveseat. "Michael and I are on the verge of breaking up. He promises to be home at a decent hour, but he never gets home before seven and sometimes it's as late as nine."

"You said that job means a lot to him. Maybe it's taking longer than he thought to get his business up and running."

"He says that all the time, but where's the mutual respect? Michael is more than I deserve, I know that, but

I thought men who loved each other made allowances for each other."

"I love you, Kid, but love isn't always a bed of roses. It can get downright messy."

His failure to support me angered me. "I thought we were friends."

"Friends tell each other the truth."

"Where's your sympathy? You've gone through shit like this and should have some advice. I hate to say it but you disappoint me." I stood to leave. "Thank you for listening."

He stopped me at the door. "You're the toughest man I know, Paul. I'll leave you with this; you will come out of whatever this is even stronger and better. Most couples go through a variation of this and most make it through."

Eddie's words gave me momentary hope, but Michael was gone and I didn't see how I would get him back.

There was so much I missed about Michael. His cockeyed smile was gone. He was one of the few people who stood up to me and I missed him calling me on my shit. Michael had been good about keeping our relationship on an even keel, even though his needs weren't being met, and now I was without an anchor. I was a sexual being and our sex was what I missed most. Michael and I got into bed at the same time and I could sense if he wanted to make love. When I sensed it, I rested the back of my hand against this thigh. I left it there because I loved the feel of him and it was my signal that I would continue touching him. I might then brush the side of my hand against his nipple or reach down and put my hand on top of his thigh. I was in no rush, and as we started kissing I got more adventurous. Michael loved it when I played with his nipples and I missed the thrill of pulling both of his nipples like holding the reins of a spirited stallion. "When you do both it completes the circuit," he would say.

I never knew where our play would go. Our love making was our mystery, our color and our air, and each time we played I thrilled at our inventiveness in the ways we took care of each other. I liked to surprise him with something I learned from a man I'd played with, and he surprised me with tricks that I had no idea where he got them but I loved surprises. Our relationship had constancy, and every time we made love, I could count on excellent sucking, ferocious fucking and some times more good things.

Other nights our play began when Michael touched me. It wasn't a fleeting touch nor was it sexual. It was just his hand cross the top of my hand or on my knee. He didn't exert any pressure but he left it there, and I knew what he meant and my cock began to swell. His touch took me to a special place where I saw magnificent buildings and felt the bristles of his beard on my back but it wasn't a physical space, it was a state of mind.

It was our space in the universe where there were no doorbells or phones, and no unwanted solicitors pounding on the door. Michael and I were the center of our universe and all that mattered was making sure Michael got every ounce of pleasure he deserved.

The flat felt empty. The fridge was empty of the food he'd made that I could nosh on whenever hunger struck. His desk was empty as was the chair in front of it where he used to sit hunched over plans for a garden. His shampoo and Gillette shaving cream are not on the side of the tub and the towel with his name on it that I gave him for Christmas was gone. I was afraid to open the closet door but I did and his row of slacks on hangers was gone. Above them the rack of shirts we shared had mine bunched to one side then a space and then the green shirt he was wearing when I saw him the first time behind the bar. Was this an evil reminder so every time I saw it I'd beat myself up for fucking up the best relationship any man could ever want?

I started going to the bars regularly and when I played with men a second time, it wasn't as much fun. I did my best to please them and they wanted to see more of me because I was good sex, but great sex for me required equals. It took a couple dates with me being the top the whole time before I started each date saying that by the end of the evening I wanted my ass played with even though no one treated it the way Michael did. Sex had to be more than just the physicality, and

I restricted my play to Bill and Jim and other men for whom sex was essential to who they were. It was usually dark when we played and I spent most of my time with my eyes closed, so it was the initial sounds my partner made that set the tone for the night and when his sound was authentic I joined him on his journey. The few total bottoms I played with were men who thought being fucked was the reason they'd been put on this earth; I couldn't slide inside them fast enough. I thought of them as my training camp; they were practice for my play with better players.

I finally had to admit playing with the most skilled players was not just feeding my ego it was filling the void Michael left. Eddie would say I should man up, but connecting with those men was better than sitting home alone. I tried staying home and not going to the bars, but that only lasted a couple weeks and one night I'd had enough of feeling sorry for myself. I read my latest find and found the story depressing, so I took off my clothes and stood in front of the mirror. Standing there I didn't see the man I was when Michael introduced me to his cabin and I saw the empty space where Michael stood. All our happiness crashed around me and all I could do was curl up on the bed and pull the pillow over my head.

When I woke, the sky was dark, so I turned on the overhead light and put on the 501s and the flannel shirt I wore the day I met Clay. This time when I stood in front of the mirror, I knew that man. I'd cared for him and shaped him into a sexually active gay man; He was the man Eddie admired and the man Bill and Jim said had promise. I knew what to do in bars, so I grabbed my Levi jacket and keys and went out to the bars and came home with a man I'd had sex with but we spent the night talking instead of having sex. That proved that without Michael I was lost. Nothing had prepared me for life without him because I expected we'd live the rest of our lives together. I didn't know what came next but I promised myself I'd never end up the sad queen who didn't know when to quit the bars.

THIRTEEN

I spent an entire afternoon going through the boxes of porno Eddie kept in the basement. Cyrus was meticulous with his cataloguing and collected porno with the same dedication to detail as the rich man who collects Rolls-Royces. I found pamphlets that were just mimeographed sheets of papers stapled together. The artwork on the covers of much of the early material was crude images of leather men and motorcycles and long-haired blond gods recumbent on lounges surrounded by barely pubic boys. To find out how Eddie's porno would fit into the collection I met with Russ Van Buskirk, the gay librarian who was helping me with the collection and described Eddie's collection.

Russ asked, "How big is it?"

"It fills a giant bookcase and probably twenty or so boxes."

"If you accept it, there won't be room for more than your current books."

"Do I detect some prudishness?"

"Heavens no, I had dirty magazines stuck under my mattress as a kid. If I were you, I'd feel responsible for collecting as many books as I could. There are more gay and lesbian books published this year than last year."

"What is it going to take? Give me the full picture."

"In short, and I'm not saying this because I'm looking for work because I love the work I do at the Main Library, but you have to treat your collection as a library and to maintain it you will need at least one full-time librarian."

"What is that person going to do?"

"Think of it this way, each book in a library has a life from the time someone purchases it to when it's catalogued, put on a shelf, and finally when its condition is so bad it needs to be replaced. Someone has to do all of that."

"But the collection is opening in just a few months."

"You have started what's essentially a library and you have to treat it like a library and you should start looking for a librarian."

"Eddie's going to pay for a storefront and he said something about archiving."

"That's just the start. I haven't even mentioned cataloguing."

"There is a lesbian couple in Florida who wants their collection to live in San Francisco and it currently takes up their home and the building next door. I have to get it because I need more lesbian books."

"Paul, you can't take books for granted. Have you ever seen the backrooms of a library? They're huge. Your collection wouldn't need that much, but you have to face the facts. Maintaining a collection is going to take staff."

"I want to save kids from going through the crap I went through coming out."

"That's all well and good but it's still a library."

That night I told Bill about what Russ said and he agreed. "Russ is right, if you want people to use your collection you have to treat it like a library, and you're going to need help. What about Clay? What's he doing?"

"He's done a great job getting donated furniture and fixtures and I can't thank Jim enough for the ways he's organized the volunteers."

"Are you willing to admit you bit off more than you can chew?"

"I don't mind putting in a few extra hours."

"Stop fooling yourself. You know you need staff."

"But that costs money."

"Do you know why so many of our organizations failed? They failed because the guy that put it together raided their bank account or they did a miserable job fundraising, in both cases the group failed because they couldn't support themselves financially. Our community seems to have an aversion to raising money. They think it's beneath them or they think asking a friend for money will end the friendship. We are not asking our friends for money, we are asking them to join us in giving the community a trove of our history, and books that will help young kids when they are coming out. The connection doesn't end when the check is written, that's just the start of a relationship with your collection. When I write my annual check to the hospital back home that treated Mom so well when she was diagnosed with cancer, I feel good about it because I made a difference for some women with cancer. Charity is basic human nature, and the men and women who give to the collection will feel good about themselves. If they have any doubts, those doubts will be dispelled when they see the storefront full of readers."

"Building relationships takes time and the opening is just months away."

"Let me talk to Jim." He left the room and I heard muffled voices in the next room. Bill came back with a smile. "We made an embarrassing bundle when we sold the last house, and Jim agreed we could use that money as start-up money for the storefront instead of buying the building we've been looking at."

"You guys would do that?"

"When you first talked about the collection I thought it was a stupid idea, but Jim jumped at the idea of having our history in one place and he got me excited. The storefront will be a milestone, and if we don't hang together we're screwed. Jim and I are not going to let your collection die."

Jim burst in the door, "I had to be here to hug you. We absolutely want to help you any way we can to get it open."

"I don't know how I can repay you guys for your generosity."

"Money's just paper. The sooner we know where we came from, the stronger our arguments that shut up the haters. We'll give you what you need to open the storefront unless you're including a pool." He laughed and poked me in the ribs.

"A pool would be nice, although I could see a lot of wet books. Thank you so much!"

"We're here for you, Paul."

FOURTEEN

I'd made great strides in the size of the collection, which contained over 500 titles. The storefront was coming along nicely, too. With the approach of the opening my thoughts were preoccupied with details and wondering where Michael was and would I ever see him again simmered in the background. I was excited about the opening until the phone call that came from the hospital back home saying Mother had died. It hadn't thought about her for years, and it took a few seconds for her death to sink in. I remembered her kindness to me as a child, but after Father's death she was a different woman who kept an impenetrable space between us. When I finally told her I was gay, she apologized for being a "bad mother" and said she'd pray for me. I never went back to Wisconsin in part because I didn't want to go through that again with her and I didn't want to sully the best time of my life.

After a long flight, I settled into a hotel. Being there in February reminded me of how isolated I felt from the rest of the world there and how friggin' cold it gets there. I called Mother's attorney and Mr. Scharski agreed to meet me the next day. I went to his office in the bank building and his receptionist, a stout woman in dark green dress with lace collar, said, "Mr. Scharski is expecting you." I entered his wood-paneled office with maroon carpeting. Mr. Scharski had aged since I knew him as a kid but he wore the same dull dark suit. His grip was firm. "Mr. Bullen. I know this is a difficult time for you. Please be seated." He pointed to a leather arm chair.

"This is a sad time and you have my condolences and Martha's."

"Thank you. You and Mrs. Scharski knew Mother many years."

"Her health was failing and your mother knew her time was short and she had me draw up this will. Would you like me to read it?"

"Please."

He withdrew a manila folder from a desk drawer and opened it. "It's pretty simple. I, Alice Connell Bullen, am of sound mind and I leave two thousand dollars to the Jansenn Pet Shelter. I leave the remainder of my estate to my son Paul Edward Bullen."

He handed me a copy of the document. "I appreciate your time on this, Mr. Scharski."

"I'm sure you want to know the distribution of the estate."

"Of course, please proceed."

He took a yellow legal sheet from the folder and scanned it, "If I include the trust your father left for you and your mother's assests that include her home and car, Mr. Bullen, you will inherit approximately three million dollars."

I was astounded. "Did you say three million dollars? That's not right. Mother was the epitome of frugal and I went to college on a scholarship."

He leaned back in his chair. "I understand your confusion. You may not know about the trust because he died so young, but your father set up a trust at your birth and it looks like it's been well managed. He stipulated that it should be used to fight injustice. He also left you this." He handed me an envelope.

The trust was in writing, though that didn't make it any more real for me. "Thank you for your time, Mr. Scharski. I need time to digest what you told me."

"Of course. If I can be of any service in the future, please feel free to contact me."

"Thank you."

Growing up, the people in our town treated the

two wealthy families who lived there with respect and they were not like the rest of us. Their kids wore the latest fashions while my clothes came from J.C. Penney. Their kids dropped names of people I didn't know but sounded important; I knew no one important. Their kids got cars in high school; I walked. Their entire families took trips to Europe while Mother and I spent a week each summer in a cabin up north. I envied them and I wanted their money. But now with money my friends would treat me differently. I wasn't sure how but I wouldn't be the same person to them. Would I be the same person to me? I hoped I'd stay the same inside but knew I would change. That night I opened the envelope. The note was simple. *You are my dream child. Live as fully as you can.*

FIFTEEN

The opening of the storefront should have been the crown jewel of all I'd done in terms of seeking out, organizing and making a space for the first collection of gay and lesbian literature but it wasn't because my heart was broken heart and Michael, wouldn't be there. Clay kept telling me to live for today and Jim said I should rejoice; and I wished I could for their sakes because they did so much work on it. They deserved to celebrate their accomplishments at a grand ceremony without the dead weight of me dragging the ceremony down.

The volunteers and their friends were already excited by the prospect of seeing the storefront open, but if I didn't perk myself up and exude the enthusiasm they expected of me, I would fail them and they would leave what should have been a grand opening a grand disappointment. Disappointment is a leitmotif of the queer history symphony and this day of all days should have been the day disappointment stops! We are a proud people, and the collection would show every lesbian and gay man they had ancestors that won wars, discovered medical cures, composed symphonies, wrote sublime poems, and created great art. When the next generation of queer kids comes to grips with their sexuality they will have books that make their coming out less painful and I shouldn't be known as the grump who spoiled the collection's opening. I told myself to celebrate, but as I poured water into the kettle I remembered Michael and how much I missed his warmth in the morning.

I got to the storefront and saw people coming from every direction and asked Clay, "Where are all these people coming from? You said you expected maybe sixty people."

"I lied and this is just the beginning. Groups in Oakland and Berkeley chartered busses.

"Why didn't you tell me? The last few weeks haven't been the cheeriest for me."

A VW Microbus with a peace symbol pulled up in front of the storefront and lesbians in dungarees got out and hailed me from the curb. Just as they began wandering around, a yellow school bus drove up and stopped in front of the storefront. It let out a busload of boisterous women and men in brightly colored clothing. Before they had been absorbed into the crowd, a second yellow bus of cheering people hanging out the windows pulled up beside the first and let loose more men and women screaming their heads off.

Clay pulled me aside. "A man needs a few surprises but this is more than I expected. Word must have really gotten out!"

"It's bigger than I imagined." I heard a familiar voice behind me.

I turned and saw Kerry. He introduced me to Ignacio, a good look man with golden brown skin and short black hair. "Sorry I haven't been in touch. I'm madly in love with this man and we're moving to Berkeley next week because Ignacio is starting graduate school at UC."

"Nice to see you've settled down, cousin."

Jeff I recognized from the party in the country walked up hand in hand with Richard. "We fell in love after that party in the country and Tim is living with us but he couldn't be here."

"Congratulations. I love seeing friends in love."

"We have to get this show on the road," Clay said as he climbed onto the small stage.

"Let's do it." I joined him on the stage, pushing aside thoughts of Michael.

Clay began, "As a native of this beloved city, it's

ironic that sixty years ago, my grandfather, Antonio Grimaldi, stood on this very spot and sold fish to the Irish Catholic mothers who fed it to their sons while today I stand on this spot an agnostic ex-Catholic son who kisses Catholic men."

The loud cheering rolled like thunder.

"I want each of you to close your eyes." He paused. "Go ahead." He paused again. "There you go. Now I want you to think of why you're here."

When I heard someone crying, I began to tear up.

"We wouldn't be here today had it not been for our faerie godfather Eddie Gillibrand. Stand up Eddie and let them see you." The crowd cheered wildly. Eddie stood and waited until they quieted. Eddie then said, "In my day what you are doing today couldn't happen; we lived in the shadows. For generations, gay men and lesbians couldn't be themselves because they lived in fear. Fear we would lose our job. Fear we'd lose our home and our family. Our biggest fear was that no one would ever truly know us. Each of you is part of a revolution that will ignite communities just like this across the country. Change comes slowly but your faces tell me that what you've started here can't be stopped. I want you to enjoy every second of this celebration, but if we are to succeed as a community know that this is just the beginning of a long, slow slog, but sixty years from now young lesbians and gay kids will look back at this time and say, 'This collection help start the revolution.'"

Eddie had put into words what so many of us were thinking. "Before I go, I want to say something about Paul. He taught me there is nothing more important than friendship. Friendships are beautiful and messy; they lift us up and they get downright awful, but they make us who we are. He showed me that without friends we are less. As you go into the world, nurture your friendships and treasure your friends because they make life worth living." Eddie sat down amidst applause.

Clay returned to the microphone. "It is now my great honor to introduce Thom Gunn, America's finest poet." Thom rose clearly uncomfortable being in front of such large crowd. He gripped the podium. "Thank you to whoever invited me." He winked at me and chuckled. "We are very lucky to be on this spit of land surrounded by the sea and bay, there is no city like San Francisco and it didn't come by its reputation easily. It took years of prostitutes pleasing their clients and vast quantities of liquor and then there was that damn earthquake, but San Francisco not just survived, it thrived because it never closed its doors to anyone. When you leave today, I want you to skip sitting on your lazy asses in front of the TV and write your own poems. I'd like to read a poem entitled, 'My Sad Captain.'" He cleared his throat and read the poem with a steady monotone. When he finished reading, he stepped back as the crowd applauded.

Clay waited for them to quiet and tapped the microphone. "Finally, he told me not do to do it, but he owes it to his fans."

There was much laughter especially from the men in the crowd.

"I want to introduce Paul Bullen. If he hadn't asked the simple question, 'Who are my gay ancestors', we wouldn't be here today. His determination to find the women and men who preceded us in history gave us the richest trove of our history. And if it weren't for something else some of you know about Paul, he'd be a very dull man indeed. Please say hi to Paul."

The crowd roared its appreciation and I fought back tears.

I stood at the podium. This was the culmination of my journey to collect and begin to preserve our history, a journey I took alone at first, but it now had a home, and for hundreds of people who were taking part of a journey they now had a home.

"Clay lied. I couldn't sit quietly and let the rest of you have all the fun. There are people I have to thank and they are the people you should be honoring today. I want to first thank Clay Grillo who is responsible for every stick of furniture in the storefront and I want to thank Jim Hickey who turned a rag-tag group of lovers into an army of volunteers who didn't let a cranky city inspector stop them from putting the memorial bricks in the entryway. Each of you is special and don't let anyone tell you otherwise. There is no one like you. Look around. Are you the boy who called you names? Are you the girl who said you weren't pretty enough to date the boys on the football team? You're not, but do you remember how much they hurt you and how bad you felt? When you think about it now, do you wonder why it even mattered? It takes more than a plane or bus ticket to come to San Francisco, because each of you had the courage to love yourself first. Each of you knew that being true to yourself risked losing friends, but you'll find in the end the friends you lost weren't true friends. Each of you should know that being here in San Francisco is a responsibility. It's my responsibility to make sure the city stays open to every lost soul and I'm responsible to every gay man and lesbian to provide them with honest information." I paused and waited for the applause to die down.

"As a kid, I wanted a wise man to suddenly appear, say a few words and everyone would love me. Guess what? It didn't happen, and it didn't happen because the people didn't know me, and they didn't know me because I never told them who I really was. Each of you is the strongest messenger of hope because only you know who you are. Telling your story to friends and family is not just right; it's a great political strategy. Each of you changes the world by simply saying the words 'I am a gay man' or 'I am a lesbian.' If a book in this collection gives you the strength to sit down with your parents and be honest about your sexuality, I will go to the great bath house in the sky a happy man. I can't thank you enough for being here today. Congratulate yourselves!"

Eddie took the microphone. "People move to New York because they aspire to be the most successful artist; they move to LA because they aspire to be the most successful movie star. But you aspired to be free to love whomever you want and that's the purest reason of all."

The crowd roared with delight.

"Now, I'm sure he'd rather be known for his 'special talents' but we are here today to honor Paul, and as you leave the men and women he found are not just his ancestors; they're *your* ancestors, too."

A clear female voice in the far back began singing "Somewhere over the rainbow ..." A male voice quickly joined her "Way up high ..." More voices joined until a chorus of hundreds sang in unison. It was the most emotional moment of my life and I couldn't stop crying.

Eddie hugged me. "You're a splendid human being and it's an honor to have you as a friend, Mr. Bullen."

"I never knew what 'friend' meant until I met you."

"Can I take you out to dinner?" Suddenly, I realized my crying had been as much about missing Michael as it was about the beauty of the ceremony.

"I need some quiet time alone." With the storefront open, I had to start the next stage of my life and I needed time to cry.

As I walked home, the dense summer fog tumbling down Twin Peaks suited the loss that was eating me from the inside. The street lamp seen through the mist told me I was at the corner. Ahead of me I saw the outline of a shrouded figure near the front of my building. Hadn't I already had a sufficient dose of misery? Was there a new threshold of pain? I cautiously inched closer and when the figure moved the hair on my arm bristled. I prepared myself to turn and run if the figure came after me. The figure pulled back the hood enough so I could see a beard and his stance didn't suggest aggression, so I approached but before I could see a face, I heard, "I was so proud of you standing there."

"I can't believe it's you?" The last person I expected to see, but the one I wanted more than anyone was standing before me.

"I love you Paul and I always have," Michael said.

"Why didn't you tell me you were there? I wanted you next to me."

"Everyone was there for *your* day, and I didn't want to disrupt it. Can I come upstairs?"

I was so dumbstruck it took me a moment to put words together. "Only if you promise me you'll stay for the rest of your life."

I threw my arms around him. "I never stopped loving you. Michael."

He took my hand, grinned, and we walked home.

SOUNDTRACK

American Pie, Don McLean
Helplessly Hoping, Crosby Stills Nash & Young
Magical Mystery Tour, The Beatles
Joy to the World, Three Dog Night
Elton John, Elton John
Johnny Mathis the Great Years, Johnny Mathis
*Procol Harum Live: In Concert with the Edmonton
Symphony Orchestra*, Procol Harum
Heart Like a Wheel, Linda Ronstadt
Nilsson Schmillson, Henry Nilsson
Grievous Angel, Gram Parsons
All I Could Do Is Cry, Etta James
Twenty Years of Dirt, Nitty Gritty Dirt Band

AFTERWARD

I grew up a bright kid in a medium-sized town in Northern Wisconsin. My goal from the start was living in a big city, but I made the mistake of attending college in an even smaller town in New Hampshire. I chose city planning for graduate work because it assured me I'd get to a big city. While I was in Philadelphia I had a ruinous affair with a man that forced me into the closet. I arrived in San Francisco in 1971 after serving as a Peace Volunteer assisting Chileans build low cost housing. A year later with my wife I moved back to the States and in 1972 with a wife, a child and a Volvo station wagon I came out. San Francisco allowed me to be me and I couldn't have asked for a better time to come out.

The inspiration for this novel is the unconditional love of Michael A. Schoch as he evolved from beloved bartender at Toad Hall to one of the most sought after landscapers in the Bay Area. He died in 1994 and he remains as much a part of me as the hands that type this afterward.

ACKNOWLEDGEMENTS

I have to thank Michael Nava for his initial support of me as a budding writer. I want to thank David Groff who saw something in my writing and was astute enough to know I needed a line editor. I want to thank Wayne Hoffman a no-nonsense guy who taught me the basics of novel writing and what punctuation means. I have to thank my readers Trebor Healey, John Killacky, Jewelle Gomez, William Johnson and Charlie Pendergast for their patience and generosity. Finally, Don Weise, my editor, deserves my thanks for initially introducing me to David and Wayne. Even more important has been Don's insistence I keep to the story line. I couldn't have asked for a better editor and pal. Thanks, Don.

Michael Samuel is my biggest cheerleader. He's formatted every draft and patiently listened to each chapter, and he'll deny it but, I wouldn't be at this point in my writing if it weren't for him. Crawford Barton's photograph is used with the permission of the Gay and Lesbian Historical Society. Much of the historical material comes from Michael Bronski's excellent *A Queer History of the United States*. (Boston. Beacon Books, 2011)

I also thank my four parents, none of whom were writers, for teaching me the importance of honesty and an inheritance that has allowed me to write without the worries of not having enough money to pay the rent.

Clay Grillo, my first boyfriend, said the universe provides. Clay was unable to save the man he loved from a long painful death and died by his own hand, but his energy lives on in my heart.

ABOUT THE AUTHOR

Chuck Forester was raised in northern Wisconsin and attended Dartmouth and Penn and holds a MCP in city planning and an MFA in poetry. He spent two years in the Peace Corp in Chile with his wife and his son was born shortly after they arrived in San Francisco in 1971. Chuck worked for three San Francisco mayors before serving as an executive with several non-profits. He was chairman of the Board of the Human Rights Campaign Committee, now the Human Rights Campaign (HRC) and he led the effort that raised $3.5 million for the Hormel Gay and Lesbian Center at the SF Public Library. Since coming out Chuck's has had a keen interest in supporting LGBT literature and preserving LGBT history.

Chuck had the good fortune to come out in 1972 in the most supportive possible environment. Michael A. Schoch, his partner of eighteen years, succumbed to AIDS in 1994. Chuck has been living with HIV since 1987.

CPSIA information can be obtained
at www.ICGtesting.com
Printed in the USA
FSOW01n0038290417
33560FS